SORCERY AND FIREDRAKES

LISA BLACKWOOD

SORCERY & FIREDRAKES

A GARGOYLE & SORCERESS TALE / BOOK 7

LISA BLACKWOOD

Sorcery & Firedrakes

Gargoyle & Sorceress Book 7

COVER DESIGNED BY: Heather Hamilton-Senter

PROOFREAD BY: Tracy Vandervliet

Special Thanks to Stan H for his eagle eyes.

PRINT ISBN: 978-1-990608-53-7

EDITION: 10/27/2021

❀ Created with Vellum

BOOKS BY LISA BLACKWOOD

Gargoyle & Sorceress

Dawn of the Sorceress

Sorceress Awakening

Sorceress Rising

Sorceress Hunting

Sorceress at War

Sorceress Enraged

Legacy of the Sorceress

Sorcery & Firedrakes

Scion of the Sorceress

Sorceress Eternal

In Deception's Shadow Series (Epic Fantasy Romance)

Betrayal's Price

Herd Mistress

Maiden's Wolf

Death's Queen

The Prince's Gryphon (forthcoming)

Ishtar's Legacy Series (Epic Fantasy Romance)

Ishtar's Blade

The Blade's Beginning (short story)

Blade's Honor

Blade's Destiny

The Blade's Shadow

First Queen of the Gryphons

The King of the Anunnaki (forthcoming)

The Anunnaki's Blade (forthcoming)

Huntress vs Huntsman (Epic Fantasy Romance)

Master of the Hunt

Night Huntress

Dragon Archer

Soul Mage (forthcoming)

Sometimes it all just goes wrong.

After the Lady of Battles orders a hopeless mission into gargoyle territory, only Captains Vaspara and Sorac survive.

Now that they have escaped and everyone back home thinks they're dead, the two captains see a once in a life-time opportunity to escape their bloody destinies.

But where can a succubus with a conscience and a firedrake who only wants to fly off into the sunset with his closest friend go to be safe?

It might be foolish to wish for a quiet life after close to two thousand years of warfare, but Vaspara is nothing if not stubborn, and together, she and Sorac are determined to start a new life elsewhere.

Unfortunately...there's just one other problem.

Sorac has a clutch of fourteen eggs hidden under the Battle Goddess's fortress, and firedrakes never abandon their young.

If they want to escape once and for all, they need to find a way to rescue his clutch.

Oh, wait...

There's a third problem.

A deadly djinn guards the nest.

SORCERY & FIREDRAKES

CHAPTER ONE

"Would you like a whip?" Sorac asked his companion as he limped along at top speed. Presently, that was piteously slow. Firedrakes weren't the fastest creatures on the ground under normal circumstances, comparable to a horse, he supposed, but with only three good legs, his pace was more of a rolling shuffle.

It was the best he could do with a mangled leg. Pain, blood loss, and battling gargoyles had depleted his reserves, both magical and physical. It would be a day or more before he could run. Longer until he was flight worthy.

He couldn't recall a time he'd been as weak.

"Would it get your big, lazy ass to move faster?" Vaspara replied in a flippant tone.

"Not unless I thought there was a reward at the end of the journey..." He gave Vaspara what would have been a lecherous look if he'd been in the form of a man.

On his saurian features, it must look humorous for she laughed.

"In your current condition, sex with me would be the last thing you ever did. Then I'd have to explain to the Battle Goddess all by myself how her force had been so soundly defeated—I can think of better ends. You damn well better live to have my back."

"Always, my sharp-tongued one."

Their banter had been much the same the last three leagues since they'd exited the portal created by Anna and Shadowlight. It had dumped them here, on the eastern border of the Battle Goddess's kingdom.

While Vaspara tried to hide her emotions behind armor, her words did nothing to disguise the stink of fear bleeding through the pores of her skin.

The stone-faced, heartless succubus captain was a disguise she wore, but deep down the thought of losing him terrified her. Her fear didn't please him, but he'd be lying if he didn't admit to being happy that she cared enough to worry.

"The valley where I stashed our servants from the blood witch isn't that much farther. They have supplies and can bind my wounds." He grunted in pain as he started up the next incline. "I heal quickly."

Thank the Divine Ones, he muttered the blasphemous statement in his own mind.

Until he healed or Vaspara had time to feed upon a male, they were both easy pickings should they encounter one of the Battle Goddess's other soldiers looking to advance themselves in the ranks.

"We're on the wrong side," Vaspara blurted.

Sorac glanced around at the mountain peaks to be sure he wasn't more confused than he'd thought. But, no, he recognized the place. "We're on the right track."

Vaspara smacked her fist against her armor-clad thigh. "No. The war."

Ah. That.

He'd thought the same thing a time or two, but as half-breeds with a dark parentage, neither he nor Vaspara would be welcomed by the Light. Not after serving the Battle Goddess for close to two thousand years. Not that they'd ever been given a chance to find a different path.

He huffed out a humorless laugh. "For what it's worth, I agree, but it's not like we had a choice."

"If we stay, we'll eventually die at the hands of the Avatars or be sacrificed to feed Captain Taryin's blood spells. Even if we managed to kill the blood witch, the Battle Goddess would be swift to kill us herself."

Sorac agreed with everything she'd just said. "But where else can a half-blood succubus and firedrake go to find a safe haven?"

"I don't know," Vaspara sighed. "But I haven't lived this long to just give up. We need to find someplace to wait out the war. This is the perfect opportunity. The gargoyles killed the rest of the company. If we don't return, the Battle Goddess will assume we have fallen along with the others. We'll never have another chance like this."

Sorac snorted in surprise. Steam and a lick of flame curled between his teeth and out his nostrils. "What you say... is correct, but it won't be easy."

"Nothing ever is."

"True." Sorac scrambled the rest of the way up the slope and then collapsed at the top. "Just like this incline isn't as easy as I thought."

"Sorac!" Vaspara called out to him as she raced up to the top and circled around in front until she could meet his gaze. Visibly relaxing, she scowled at him to hide her feelings. "Damn it to the void. Don't scare me like that again."

He tried to get to his feet.

"No! Stay down! Don't move. I'll share power with you, and then you *will* shift back into a man. I need to apply new bandages to your leg. That task will be easier if you're man-sized when I do it."

"I'll shift," Sorac said guardedly, "but you can't spare the magic. I feel how depleted you are already."

"Stop whining. We're doing this." Vaspara placed her hands upon his chest. Immediately her power ran along his skin. "Lower your shields you fool! Or I'll just be wasting magic."

There was no fighting Vaspara once she'd set her mind to something, so he did as she ordered while secretly basking in her attention. Once he'd absorbed enough magic, he triggered his shift. Soon his body was shrinking, his wings retracting.

When it was done, he felt lightheaded but was a man again. His enchanted armor had even made the shift with him. He hadn't been sure the metal still possessed enough magic after the battle.

"Good. Stay down." Vaspara swiftly removed his shin guards and then unlaced both boots and pulled them off before reaching for his belt. Even though he knew it wasn't what it looked like, a grin spread across his face. "Knew it. You're hungry and frantic to get me naked."

"Keep dreaming. I don't care how nice your package is. The fertility god heritage is an enormous drawback. Absolute deal breaker."

Sorac continued to grin up at her as she unbuckled his belt and pulled it off. For fifteen hundred years, he'd been dreaming of bedding Vaspara, but he wanted more than that. She was the one he wanted to raise his brood.

Unaware of his thoughts, she set aside the belt and moved to the remaining armor encasing his leg. She freed it a piece at a time. Not an easy or pain-free task with his leg broken in three places.

Once the armor was off, she used her dagger to slit his pants from leg to boot cuff and then gently pulled aside the blood-soaked leather.

He grinned at her. "I liked those pants."

"And I'd like you to live, so just lie there and keep your mouth shut."

Sorac continued to grin as her warm fingers gently probed his ankle, working her way up. If it weren't for the agonizing pain each time she found a fracture, he would have savored the feeling of her fingers upon his flesh.

"Your touch almost makes the broken bones worth—" His half playful words ended in a scream as she shifted bones back into alignment.

"Sorry." Vaspara smirked, ruining her apology.

"By the Mother Goddess, next time warn me before you do that!"

Smiling innocently, Vaspara continued her examination of his leg. "I find it's better if the patient does not know it's coming."

A second snarl of pain escaped him as she set the next break. By the time she'd finished splinting and tightly wrapping the entire length of his leg, a fresh layer of sweat covered his body, and he shook like a newborn foal.

Vaspara retrieved a water skin from one of their packs.

"Here, sip this." She held it out to him, and he drank thirstily. "Easy. Not so much at one time."

Once he'd had as much as he dared, he leaned back and rested against the ground. He resisted the urge to close his eyes. If he surrendered to sleep, there was no guarantee he'd live to wake. A patrol might come upon them while he was senseless. He could sleep later. They needed to be farther away from the fortress.

Trying to ignore the demands of his exhausted body, he looked up at the succubus instead. Her vizor was up, and dark bags under her eyes showed against her pale skin. Gods, her complexion was almost grey. Dirt or a bruise lay like a smear of soot across one high cheekbone. Her blonde braid had escaped from inside her helmet and thumped against her breastplate. The ends were a rusty red from dried blood. More gore splattered her armor.

She looked about as bad as he felt.

"Thank you for not abandoning me, Vaspara."

"You've never deserted me."

"I'll never leave your side as long as I draw breath." *And there I go sounding like a lovelorn youth after his first sighting of a succubus.*

But Vaspara didn't roll her eyes or unleash some sarcastic remark about idiot lizards. Leaning forward, her face came into focus, and he saw the shimmer of tears in her eyes. One of her hands came up to cup his face, and she pressed a kiss to his forehead. "Keep drawing breath, you fool. I don't know what I'd do without you."

Then the Captain Vaspara he'd known for over a thousand years returned, chasing away that other, soft-hearted female who had touched his face so gently.

"Come on," she barked. "We need to keep moving, or we'll never reach the camp before dark, and it looks like a storm is brewing."

Sorac struggled to obey, but she had to help hoist him up and then support most of his weight. He wouldn't have been able to move on his own.

"Leave me," he urged. "If you and the servants leave now, you have a chance to put a good bit of distance between yourselves and the goddess's patrols."

"I'm not leaving you." She rolled her eyes at him this time.

"Once I'm healed, I can take to the wing to catch up." He didn't mention the outcome would depend on if the patrols found him before he healed.

"I'm not leaving you," she growled. "You can't even walk. There's no way you can protect yourself. Now shut up and let's get to the servants' camp. Once we get a couple of meals in you and rest, we'll be in better shape to make life-changing decisions."

"You can't protect me, lovely Vaspara, not without first feeding, and I'm the only male here."

"I will not feed from you. You're too weak as it is. We'll make do."

Now that the severity of his condition was setting in, he worried; though, not for himself. If he was to die, so be it. He'd won hundreds of battles in his lifetime. There was no shame in being defeated by overwhelming numbers of worthy enemies, and any gargoyle was a worthy opponent.

But Vaspara still had a chance.

"I want you to leave me behind," he begged one last time. "If I'm found, I'll tell the others you were injured, and I was too weak to feed you, that you died."

"Shut up and come with me."

"Why is it so important to you?" he asked, though he was sure he already knew the answer.

"Because I love you!" She screamed the words and then fell silent.

Shocked by her outburst? Or perhaps the words themselves?

"Vaspara, I—"

"I'm not leaving you behind." Her eyes locked on his, her expression fierce and determined. "You can just shut up and walk. If not, I can club you over the head and carry you."

Suddenly, he needed to tell her how he felt. If he died without admitting his feelings, it would eat away at his spirit for eternity.

"I've loved you for over a thousand years." He stroked his knuckles against her cheek, and something else occurred to him. "That was far too long to make me wait to hear you feel the same way."

"Move, or they'll be the last words you ever hear." Vaspara's tone might be harsh, but she was as gentle as possible as she helped him along the path.

Goddess, her sharp words always made him hard. Not that he was in any shape to do anything. Just then he jarred his broken leg and winced, which helped to cool his blood.

Together they shuffled to their destination.

CHAPTER TWO

Bleeding blight and damnation! She'd lost her mind and told the firedrake her feelings. There was no way to take her words back, and he'd been swift to confirm he felt the same way. That was so very dangerous for them both. They didn't have time for emotional complications while they were still fleeing for their lives.

Perhaps in a few years, if they survived that long and found a place to hide, maybe then they could revisit this situation with their disturbing emotions. But there was another concern, wasn't there? Sorac couldn't just up and flee their old home as easily as she could.

"Even if we escape and heal, we can't just run off with no plan." Vaspara frowned at the trail ahead, scanning for dangers even as she mulled over possibilities in her mind. "There are other considerations. Your brood for one."

Sorac stared at her with a shocked expression. "You know about them?"

"I make it my business to know everything there is to know about my fellow captains."

In truth, she'd only found out about his brood fifty years ago. He'd kept that secret well-guarded until then.

"How?" he asked at last.

"You slept with a soldier under my command. Got her pregnant." Vaspara huffed. "Brakaya couldn't train during that time. Annoyed me more than a little."

"Sorry," Sorac coughed. "Shouldn't have poached from your ranks."

"No, you shouldn't have, but you were also my friend, and you always seemed like the fatherly type, so I told Brakaya there'd be a big promotion if she didn't rid herself of it."

"Ah. I wondered why she'd been so eager to keep it. I didn't have to promise her as much as I'd thought."

"Worked both angles for the best payout, did she?" Vaspara snorted. "Anyway, imagine my surprise when she presented me with an egg three months later. I told her to take it to you upon threat of death. At which point I followed in secret to make sure she obeyed and then later, I followed you to the cavern under the Battle Goddess's temple."

"You saw my nest?"

She nodded. "The succubus's egg was number fourteen."

"Yes." Sorac cleared his throat. "The unplanned one."

"Hmm. Tall. Blonde. Big breasts. Succubus. Sound like someone you know?" Vaspara could have been describing herself. Sorac had picked a female who looked as much like her as he could find.

"It wasn't actually intentional," Sorac stared ahead, but Vaspara didn't miss the bloom of blood under the tracery of fine scales covering his skin. "Had too much to drink when I was cycling."

Vaspara snorted. Although she was sure he was telling the truth. Mixed heritage sometimes caused unforeseen complications as she could attest to. She'd known Sorac for a very long time and knew he hated one aspect of his dual natures.

He went into heat once every hundred years. She wasn't sure if it was his firedrake nature or that of a fertility god that triggered his cycle.

"I normally arrange it with a willing female from a battalion under my command and enlighten her to everything that will happen. I also make sure the female has no interest in raising the child."

Scales, shoulder spikes, and all, Sorac was one of the finest-looking males she'd ever laid eyes on. It wouldn't take much convincing for a woman to fall into his bed. It probably didn't take that much more to convince a few ambitious types to gestate an egg, especially if they didn't have to raise the firedrake's young afterward. But what was the point of collecting a big clutch of eggs and never hatching them?

"Why the stipulation the female have no interest in the egg after she's... birthed it?"

"Two reasons. First, if everyone thinks I'm simply disposing of unwanted offspring, then no one will think to look for my nest to use as collateral. Safer for both myself and my unhatched little ones. And second," he glanced sharply at her, "why would I want to raise my drakelings with a woman I don't love? My nature may force me to copulate with a random female once a century, but I'll be the one to pick my brood's mother."

"This is a firedrake thing, isn't it?"

"Yes." He hissed in pain as he put too much weight on his bad leg, but after a moment he continued his explanation. "I normally arrange everything well in advance."

"What happened that last time?"

"I was tired of being coerced by my nature and decided to be stubborn."

"Didn't work so well?"

"No. I tried to drink myself under the table for the duration of the cycle, but at one point I sobered up enough to come to seek you out."

Vaspara felt something strange stir in her middle. "You never made it though, did you?"

"No. When I reached your chambers, you were with another male, feeding." Unhappiness flashed across his face before he glanced uphill at the terrain still ahead.

Vaspara felt an echoing resonance deep in her soul. Sorac had needed her, and she hadn't been there for him. It was a useless feeling because even if he'd come to her, she couldn't have given him what he needed. As a captain in the Battle Goddess's army, having a child was the fastest way to get a demotion. Not to mention making her vulnerable to her enemies.

All the same, she still felt like she'd let the firedrake

down. He'd always had her back and had helped her out of a few scrapes in her time. Once, after a particularly brutal battle with a gargoyle patrol, she'd been too injured to make it back to camp and Sorac had hunted until he found her even though he'd sustained wounds himself.

When he'd seen she was in no shape to travel any farther without feeding, he'd gone back to camp to collect one of her male soldiers and flown the man to her side. Sorac had then stayed and guarded her until she'd fed and recovered.

There had been several other times throughout their lives they'd saved each other. That had forged a powerful bond between them.

"I'm sorry I wasn't there to find someone better to assuage your need," she muttered.

"Don't be. We are both ruled by our natures." Sorac sighed. "The other succubus used her magic. I wasn't in any state to resist."

"It doesn't surprise me Brakaya waylaid you. She and I were in competition for many years. Sleeping with one of the captains is very prestigious. Plus, she hated me and knew you and I were friends. She likely thought she was stealing you away." Vaspara snorted with dark humor. "She was probably bitterly regretting that decision in the middle of popping out that egg."

"Most likely. Normally I go to the female when the egg is near term and use my magic to remove it from her painlessly."

Morbid curiosity stirred. "I know you didn't offer Brakaya that same option, why?"

He grunted, but she didn't think it was from the patch of rough terrain they were crossing.

At last, he drew in a deep breath and answered. "She took my choice away. I wouldn't have been feeling particularly forgiving under normal circumstances, but then that next morning she gloated."

When he glanced at Vaspara, she found herself momentarily mesmerized by the red of his elemental fire lighting a bright ring around his irises. His voice when he continued was a low growl. "She claimed she was a more skilled lover than you. More skilled in all things. She would continue to warm my bed if I helped her displace you as leader of your battalion."

Vaspara grinned at him. "What did you do to her?"

"There may have been threats that if something happened to you, I'd eat her and not in the way she'd enjoy."

"Hmm, that must have been around the time she stopped being a thorn in my side."

"Well, at least that night resulted in something beneficial."

There was that, she supposed.

Talking seemed to help take Sorac's mind off his pain. She scrounged for something else to talk about, but her mind kept circling back to his brood.

"Eggs. How is that even possible with a female who's not a firedrake?"

"I admit, that was a surprise the first time. I later asked the eldest of the herb witches what they knew about firedrakes. It seems male firedrakes produce unique egg-seeds.

Once they enter a womb, they seek the female's eggs and swallow any they find. Once a female egg is fertilized, the remaining mass from the male seed later grows into the egg's shell."

Vaspara made a face. "Swallows the female's egg... I'm visualizing little monsters swimming around in your man-jizzrile devouring everything in their path. I'm never having sex with you."

"You asked." His laugh soon turned into a groan.

"How much farther?" she asked, feeling a renewed spike of concern for him. She was still sharing magic to keep him going, but she didn't have much more to offer.

"Almost there." He sounded as relieved as she felt.

Eventually, they reached their destination. The structures were so well disguised by vines and branches Vaspara hadn't even spotted the makeshift shelters until two of Sorac's servants called a soft greeting. Callum, Sorac's manservant, and Sylas, the human's fifteen-year-old son, came forward and took the firedrake from Vaspara.

Soon the rest of their servants were rushing forward, exclamations of concern and demands to know what had happened on their lips.

Mattis, Vaspara's oldest and most trusted servant, limped through the small crowd, growling out orders for calm. Once peace was restored, he came to stand next to Vaspara.

"Sorac's a tough bastard. He'll pull through," Mattis said as he watched other members of his family aid the firedrake's servants prepare food, medicine, and a place for him to rest.

At the sound of his calm confidence, Vaspara relaxed. She trusted Mattis almost as much as Sorac. The spry grandfather had once been one of her lovers many, many years ago until he'd proven much more valuable for his wise counsel than any momentary benefits she gained from a feeding.

Only when the servants had a spot prepared in one of the shelters did Vaspara sever the link she'd forged to share power with Sorac. The drain on her depleted magic stopped, but the sudden lack left her feeling more than a little useless, but she still followed the others into the vine-covered tent.

Taking up a position along one fabric wall, she stood like a silent sentinel as Alaya, Mattis's daughter-by-marriage, who was a competent herb witch, began tending to Sorac's injuries.

CHAPTER THREE

Sorac jerked awake. Immediately he cataloged his surroundings. A tent canvas rippled above his head, and the breeze carried distant voices to him. Someone had covered him head to toe in a heavy blanket.

When he moved, his leg ached but was quickly forgotten when he discovered he wasn't alone in the makeshift camp bed. Another warm, living weight was beside him under the blanket. Pushing aside a corner, he gazed upon Vaspara's long blonde hair. She was tucked up against his side, her one arm draped across his chest.

She was still fully clothed, minus her armor, but that didn't seem to deter his body, which was ready for her. Closing his eyes again, he relaxed back against his pillow and drew Vaspara more firmly against his side. She didn't even stir at his touch or at being shifted.

More than a thousand years he'd waited for this instant. A grin spread across his face, then quickly faded.

Knowing Vaspara, the moment wouldn't last. As soon as she woke, she'd immediately leave the bed and never comment on the reason she'd crawled under the blanket with him.

If he let her.

His brows drew together, and a smirk touched his lips.

He would not let things return to the way they'd been.

Vaspara had admitted her feelings yesterday, and that changed everything. Now he saw the potential for a bright new future for the two of them and his brood.

The reason he'd fought tooth and claw to gain his position and survive all the horrors he'd seen in his life was because of this woman in his arms and his precious brood of fourteen eggs still back in the fortress. Only having his clutch here with them could have improved this moment.

He wasn't a fool. Rescuing his clutch wouldn't be easy. Although it might prove much easier than convincing Vaspara she'd be the perfect mother for his brood.

"I love a good challenge," he whispered into her hair, "and the reward for success will be like nothing I've experienced before."

Beside him, Vaspara shifted, and a soft, sweetly endearing snort escaped her. After a moment, her fingers flexed against his naked chest in a small caress.

The next moment a small grunt of pain escaped Vaspara as she lifted her head from his chest. He drew in a surprised breath. Her skin was almost grey, and the bags under her eyes looked like day old bruises.

"Vaspara why haven't you fed yet?" He reached out and touched her papery skin and then her hair, which felt as coarse as straw, nothing like its usual silky texture. Her skin even seemed to sag from her bones.

"I couldn't leave you, not when you were so weak." Her fingers flexed against his skin as hunger entered her gaze, but she still didn't initiate a feeding even though she desperately needed to.

"Silly succubus," he purred as he stroked her hair from her cheek. "Let me provide you with what you need. I swear there is no danger." Then with a chuckle, he added, "I won't even get you pregnant."

His lips found hers, and she moaned in desperation and hunger. Soon she was kissing him harder, the caress of lips on lips punishing and devastating and delightful at the same time. Her hands settled to grip the spikes on his shoulders where his scales were longer and tougher.

As her lips broke their kiss to trail down his throat, he felt the moment she fed on him. She was still fully clothed, and already his power rose in answer to her need, feeding her his love along with his desire.

For her, this would only be sex. He knew it, and he was fine with that. They had all their lives ahead of them. That was time enough for this to become something more profound. This time, he was merely happy to provide her with something she needed.

Suddenly she shuddered and drew back, her lips breaking away from his.

"What's wrong?" he asked as he gently smoothed a hand down her back. "Why did you stop feeding?"

"I can't do this." One hand came up to caress his brow,

her fingers stroking higher to the crown of bone at the base of his short horns. "You're too weak. I won't see you set back your healing. I'll go find a servant."

"No, you won't." He drew her back down until they were again pressed tight together. "You're too weak. I'm not letting you out of my sight. Take what I offer. There is no risk of you getting pregnant, I promise."

"I don't want to hurt you."

"You won't. My power is the opposite of yours. I grow stronger with the giving of passion. The more pleasure we share, the stronger we'll both grow." His words seemed to sink in for she stopped resisting and pressed herself back against him, latching on to his mouth as if she planned to suck out his soul.

Mentally smirking, he admitted there was something else he'd love to surrender to the suction of her lips, but that could wait until after she'd recovered.

"Clothes off," he ordered and helped her when her limbs were too weak to manage it on her own. Soon she was as naked as he. Stroking his hands over her skin, he marveled at the silky bounty that was his to explore. Each touch and caress seemed to rejuvenate her a little more, and soon she was touching him in return.

Sometime later, he grimaced and muttered a swift warning when her greedy fingers nearly had him spilling in their clasp.

Vaspara's expression softened. "How long has it been?"

"Years."

"Years?!" She parroted.

"Four years. Last time some fool challenged me for my title. I was injured. Not unlike a succubus, sex speeds my healing and replenishes my magic." He cupped her face and caressed her bottom lip, gently exposing her sharp fangs. His firedrake nature wanted her to use them on his body. "I stopped wanting other women a very long time ago. Only my hundred-year fertility cycle could sway me. It's another firedrake thing, I think."

"But I've seen you ogle females often enough, even pursue them, making jokes about finally catching and bedding them. You're not exactly subtle in your lusts."

"A deception to hide how I felt about you. Love is perceived as a weakness; you know that." He gave her a sad smile. "The reputation about how my seed always strikes true usually keeps unwanted females running in the opposite direction. It was very handy unless I actually needed to bed a woman."

"Well, you seem to want me, and I have zero interest in running at this exact moment, so I'll make sure you're good and healed by the time I'm done with you."

Vaspara, normally so fierce in battle and daily life, now showed him a rare gentleness as she rose up and then slowly straddled him, being careful not to jar his leg or put too much pressure on any of the other bruises and wounds covering his body.

While this gentle Vaspara threatened to bring him to his end far too soon, the tender look in her eyes soothed any worries he might have about not being the legendary lover she deserved. There would be time for that later.

Now there was only Vaspara above him, touching him,

urging him on with a gentleness that likely surprised her as much as him. He didn't want it to end, but like all things, this too had an ending. Afterward, he gathered her in his arms and cuddled her close as his eyelids grew heavy.

"Sleep well, my oldest and most dear friend," Vaspara whispered against his ear as he drifted off.

CHAPTER FOUR

And just like that, a succubus was ruined for life, Vaspara thought sourly. The sex probably wasn't even that great by their usual standards with neither of them at their best, but the power raised between them was the purest, sweetest substance she'd ever tasted. There was no musky or bitter taint. It was strong and clean and rejuvenating.

She wanted to taste it again already, to caress, nibble, and lick every bit of his exposed skin.

Sighing out a mournful sound, she rolled off him, being careful not to jolt his injured leg. She settled beside him on the narrow sleeping pallet. Slowly, her mind rallied as thoughts became less sluggish.

Her eyes narrowed in thought. He damn well better have been correct about not being fertile. It was bad enough that as a half-fertility deity he could make a barren woman's womb fertile. If he was ever fertile at the same time as her...

Goddess! Just imagine it! She'd make a terrible mother.

She was probably safe from that, but there were other concerns. This couldn't happen again. He was in love with her. She had a rule about that. She didn't sleep with men who fancied themselves in love with a succubus. It was too much of a nuisance.

But Sorac was different, wasn't he? As a half-blood fertility god, he was usually immune to a succubus's powers.

That meant his emotions for her were as real as the blood flowing through her body.

He loved her. Truly loved her. It wasn't her powers making him think that.

In the end, it didn't matter, though, did it? If he loved her, he'd want more from her than just her love in return.

He'd already hinted at that with the comment about only wanting to raise his drakelings with a woman he loved.

There was no way Vaspara was becoming anyone's mother. Certainly not the mother to fourteen firedrakes. And it didn't matter if it was her oldest, most trusted friend and confidant asking. The answer was still a deafening no.

"You look troubled." Sorac's sleep-roughened voice filled the tent.

She'd thought he'd fallen asleep after they'd fed. Vaspara glanced toward the bed in time to see him toss back the blanket.

"Oh, no you don't!" Vaspara was at his side in a

moment, pushing him back down, preventing him from getting up. "You need rest. Go back to sleep."

"I feel much better. Now tell me what is bothering you."

She didn't want to talk about the real reason for her disquiet, so instead, she told him something else, a secret that had been eating at her for ages. Now seemed like as good a time as any to confess.

"The Lady of Battles told me something about your heritage and then swore me to secrecy."

"Go on."

"It's about your father." Vaspara glanced down at her hands.

"Don't feel guilty about whatever secret the Battle Goddess forced you to keep from me. I'm not foolish or naïve. I know she would have killed you, or worse, for breaking confidence with her." Sorac propped himself up on his elbows to watch her. "But now it's just you and me. No secrets, so spit it out."

"You have the potential to become a demigod, one far more powerful than your father. You don't need worshipers to survive, but if you drew worshippers to you, your power could grow to rival what the Lady of Battles commands."

Vaspara allowed that to sink in. "Normally, the Battle Goddess would never have allowed a possible rival to live. The only reason she made an exception with you is because of your mother's loyalty and the rarity of firedrakes."

Sorac's mother was a rare case. Bervicta's great grandmother, an ancient harpy crone by the name of Brasscid, found a firedrake's nest. A rockslide had destroyed all but one egg.

"Captain Brasscid returned to the Battle Goddess with the egg, hatched it, and raised the firedrake chick."

"My mother, Soralia. Who later had me," Sorac agreed. "I've heard the stories of how she grew in power and became a ferocious warrior, eventually rising to the top and becoming Commander. She even apprenticed Gryton for a few centuries before she died having me."

"Don't get all teary-eyed over your mother. I knew Soralia for a time when I was younger. She was one scary drake. And she was loyal to the Battle Goddess. If your mother had lived, she would have seen to the Battle Goddess's dream of a winged battalion of firedrakes. Your mother would have spawned many clutches of eggs, but I doubt she would have seen them as anything more than tools. She was always so cold. Cruel, even by our standards."

Sorac grunted. "I've always figured I must take after my father, at least in personality."

"Yes." Vaspara grinned, still feeling the pleasant buzz from feeding. "Perhaps in more ways than just a personality."

An answering seductive smile spread across Sorac's face. "If you'd like, we can explore mo—"

Vaspara cut him off with a laugh. "I believe I was in the middle of a confession. Where was I? Ah, right. Your father destroyed the Battle Goddess's plans for Commander Soralia. It was during one of the empire's expansion phases, when the Lady of Battles sent her commander and army out to other worlds, seeking new species to strengthen our numbers."

Sorac fluffed the stuffed sack that was his pillow and then reclined with his hands tucked behind his head. The position had allowed his blanket to slip low around his waist. When he winked at her, she rolled her eyes and then collected her thoughts.

"Commander Soralia led her troops to a new world. The citizens were deemed too weak to serve in the demigoddess's army and were killed, their livestock and fields harvested to feed the dark kingdom. But your father also lived on that world. He woke from a long slumber to find his people already slaughtered or dying. In a rage, he attacked our army. Many were killed, but he was no match for Commander Soralia and all the captains. At least not in battle."

Vaspara retrieved a pitcher of water and the two cups a servant had left for them. After pouring Sorac and herself a drink, she continued her tale.

"He wasn't a warrior, but as a fertility deity, he was without compare. He turned that power into a weapon, enchanting the entire army, overwhelming them with lust. Then he ensured each joining resulted in a life being conceived that day."

Sorac shifted to fold his arms across his chest. Humor had fled his expression. "Fertility as a weapon? I would never have thought to use that power in such a way."

"But your father did, and his last great act was to beget a child—his only child—upon Commander Soralia. He endowed you with all his powers. Yet as a half-breed fire-drake you would never need worshipers to survive."

Vaspara drained her cup and set it aside. "With his temples destroyed and his worshipers slaughtered, he faded, but even then, I think he knew his vengeance would be far-reaching."

"I had no idea my father did all that." Sorac stared down into his cup, his expression blank. "All I was ever told was that he was a defeated fertility god. I assumed my mother had just thought him pretty and used him to beget me before having him killed."

Vaspara reached out and touched his shoulder. "Your father was strong, never a victim. His actions had long-lasting consequences upon the Battle Goddess's army, for he hadn't just ensured that all the females would leave the field of battle with pups in their bellies, he imprinted a strong maternal drive in each of them. They would not rid themselves of the unwanted new life. They would fight to keep them."

With one more squeeze to his shoulder, she explained the last bit of revenge the fertility god had set into motion. "Your father had left the Lady of Battles with two choices. Refrain from further battles until half her army had whelped and raised their young. Or weave a spell that would rid them of the unwanted offspring which might lead to a civil war where she could find half her army rising up against her, seeking revenge."

Sorac grinned suddenly. "My father died, but he still beat the Lady of Battles at her own game. She could do nothing to undo what he'd created that day."

"You are correct. Even the Lady of Battles admitted a mere fertility deity had defeated her. With no other viable choice, she allowed the women of her army to birth and raise their young in peace."

Rolling the water around in his cup, Sorac still didn't bother looking up as he answered her. "I always wondered why there were so many children my exact age when I was growing up. I assumed the Battle Goddess had put out an order for her army to increase its numbers naturally."

"No. She wasn't so foolish to set into motion something that would force her army to choose between duty and family."

Sorac grunted. "You speak of this all as if you were there."

Vaspara tilted her head. "Because I was."

"Yet you don't have a child." His gaze darted to her waist before returning to stare at his cup. Then, his voice gentle, he asked, "Did you lose it?"

"There never was a child." At the time, she'd just been relieved. It wasn't until later that she realized the lack of a child was partly why she'd risen to power so quickly. "Your father's magic flowed over me but didn't incite my lusts. Perhaps he didn't think a succubus would make a good mother."

Looking up from his cup, Sorac's eyes narrowed, studying her as if seeing her for the first time. "And yet, I grew up with other succubus children. They must have been conceived during that time."

She shrugged. "Perhaps there's something wrong with

me that even he couldn't fix. Or he found me wanting in some other way."

Or he knew, even as I do, that I'd be a terrible mother.

"Perhaps," Sorac agreed distractedly, his gaze distant as his thoughts turned inward.

He suspected something else though. She was certain.

"What else has been kept from me?" Sorac asked suddenly.

"Your father had one other bit of vengeance planned for Commander Soralia. As you developed, you drained all your mother's resources, stealing them for yourself so you would be powerful from the moment of your birth. Your father never wanted you to be a slave to the Lady of Battles."

"My mother wasn't killed in battle before I hatched, was she?"

"No. That was another lie the Battle Goddess ordered you be told."

Sorac drew in a deep breath and then exhaled it slowly. "I killed my mother."

"No." Vaspara was beside him again, her hand touching his. "You didn't kill your mother. Your father's spell greatly weakened her. Later, after she'd laid you, the Battle Goddess had her killed, saying no weak creature would raise one of her future captains."

The muscles along his jaws flexed. "Thank you for sharing all this with me. I knew that I'd been born of Commander Soralia and a fertility deity, but I wasn't aware of the grand scope of the deception."

"No, the Lady of Battles didn't want you to know of the

depth of your father's power. If he'd known of the impending invasion and had time to ready his people, he might have repelled our army."

"All this time, the Lady of Battles must have distrusted me for what I am, who my father was. I'm surprised I'm still alive." Sorac grunted unhappily. "I think I just pieced together something that's been bothering me. Normally, the Battle Goddess punishes her captains with a demotion if they beget young without her express command. I assumed she was granting me leniency because the heat cycles were beyond my control. And if I didn't go into nesting mode to hatch the eggs, it wouldn't impact my duties and loyalties as a captain. But that wasn't the reason at all."

"No," Vaspara agreed. "Even though you posed a risk, she still wanted you to create as many eggs as possible. After the death of your mother, the Battle Goddess saw you as her only chance to get her winged, fire breathing warriors. And as long as she had your eggs, she could ensure your loyalty in the interim."

"And after I'd hatched the eggs, reared my drakelings, and they were old enough to protect themselves? What then Vaspara?" Sorac sat up, tossing the blankets aside and faced her, no longer hiding his emotions. They burned along with the elemental fire swirling around the outer ring of his irises. "Did she already have planned out another way to control me?"

"Yes." Vaspara broke his gaze to stare at a point over his shoulder, pretending interest in the fabric walls of the tent.

"She knew I'd fallen in love with you and would have

used you to control me." His words were tired, not accusing.

"Yes." Vaspara snorted out a humorless laugh. "But in her arrogance, she miscalculated. It never occurred to her that my loyalty to you would grow stronger than my loyalty to her."

"We're both lucky to have survived this long."

It was true. No point in denying it. "Yes. Though, I think it's in part because it never occurred to her that one of her inner circle would betray her. At least not until River turned traitor to save Shadowlight, and later Gryton's defection. Now she's looking everywhere for betrayal. It was only a matter of time before she looked upon us and decided our loyalty to each other was too dangerous to allow."

"All the more reason for us to leave this land forever."

"Yes. After we rescue your eggs." Vaspara grinned savagely. "I'm possessive, and there's no way I'm leaving something that's so much a part of you behind."

"Possessive can be fun." Sorac made a deeply male sound of pleasure and tried to draw her down onto the bed with him.

"We'll discuss that later," Vaspara said as she slipped out of his grasp, intentionally not giving him a chance to get a word in. "You need to rest. I'll go speak with Mattis and tell him to pack. We can't stay here."

She turned her back on the firedrake and brushed aside the curtain suspended across the tent's opening. Dawn was painting the sky to the east in shades of pink.

CHAPTER FIVE

Sorac woke with a soft hiss. Glancing around the shelter, he discovered he was still alone. Although, Vaspara's scent still clung to his skin, and that was a rather pleasant way to wake up. Stretching again, he briefly debated staying in bed until his succubus returned, but just then his stomach growled.

Sighing, he at last rolled out of bed, dressed, and then emerged from the tent. His stomach growled again.

He'd only taken a dozen steps when the oldest of Vaspara's servants spotted him. Mattis's gait was worse than it had been last time Sorac had seen him.

"Lizardman, I see the mistress hasn't fucked you to death yet. Suppose that's good." The elder's expression gave nothing away.

"Randy old bastard, you're still alive?" Humor colored his tone, and he grinned at their familiar banter. Mattis always kept a severe expression on his face while Sorac, more often than not, ended up dissolving into merry laughter until tears rolled down his face.

With a gruff curse, Mattis reached out and drew Sorac in for a rough embrace before shoving him back to arm's length. His ancient frame still had surprising strength for one so frail looking. "Missed you and the mistress. Glad to have you back."

"I am glad to see you and the others. Living conditions haven't been too hard?"

"Ha! It's colder than a witch's teat at night, but it's better than being eaten by the blood witch. I'll live in a tent for however long I need if it keeps my family safe. Thank you for flying us all here, Lizardman."

Sorac had known the elder since birth. Same with his father before him and his grandmother before that, generation after generation stretching back a thousand years, to a time when he'd carried this man's very pregnant ancestor from a burning house after the army had rolled through her kingdom.

At the time, Sorac hadn't needed another servant, but he knew Vaspara's old, childless servants could use the help and the pregnant woman had been too lovely to allow death or a harsher master to claim her.

Seeing the subsequent generations born, grow, have children of their own, and then age until they grew old and grey was both sad and yet rewarding, too. These people might be servants, but they were as close as either he or Vaspara had to a loving family.

Thus, the reason he'd risked his life to save them from Blood Witch Taryin.

"We're not going back," he blurted suddenly.

Mattis was silent for a moment and then reached out and patted him on the arm. "Finally came to your senses, did you? I don't care if I must sculpt the walls of my house out of snow. Anything is better than returning to the fortress while that blood witch dwells there."

"I can't say I disagree with you. Gryton's defection has unbalanced the Lady of Battles, and now Taryin has summoned a Djinn." Sorac only shook his head. "And we've just returned from having our backsides soundly beat by Anna Mackenzie and a fully matured Shadowlight. I don't know what Lord Death has been up to, but there were also many warrior dryads among his young gargoyles. Things aren't like they used to be."

"Warrior dryads? Were they pretty with big," Mattis made a motion of cupping imaginary breasts. "If so, there are worse ways to die than being killed by a beautiful woman."

"Yes, they were all lovely." Sorac grinned. "However, since I'm certain they were all daughters of gargoyles, they likely had big, scary fathers and brothers who might break every bone in your body if you ogled their daughters and sisters."

"Aw, in that case. Never mind. My eyesight's fading, anyway."

Sorac just shook his head again. "Vaspara and I both feel we are on the losing side of the coming conflict. If the Avatars and their allies don't kill us, the blood witch will use us to fuel her spells with the Battle Goddess's blessing."

Mattis grunted. "Sounds like it's long past time to leave."

"I've been thinking that way since the Lady of Battles first captured the female half of the Avatars. Every time I looked into that ancient child's eyes, I swear I flinched. Now there's a djinn. The Lady of Battles has completely come unhinged."

"Lizard, you're just realizing that now?"

"No, but we've just been handed the perfect opportunity to finally escape without being noticed. Everyone thinks we're dead and that you and the other servants have long since been killed to fuel one of the witch's blood spells," he said. "Vaspara and I will find a safe place to start a village far from this land; hopefully, we will get ourselves so lost no one ever comes looking for us again. We want to bring you and the others with us."

"I like how you think, Lizard."

"You know I hate cooking, and poison might be more palatable than Vaspara's attempts." He leaned back against the tree as he looked around the clearing. "Have you seen where Vaspara went? We need to discuss something."

"Going to rescue your brood?"

Sorac choked on spit. "Has everyone figured out my secret?"

"Vaspara told us you both needed to go back for something. When I asked what could be so important to be worth risking your lives, she told me. She also told me if you don't return by a specified time, we are to leave here at once."

"Wise," he admitted. The thought of failure sobered him up from being drunk on Vaspara's essence.

Mattis jerked his chin to the next nearest cooking fire. "Here comes the mistress now."

He turned to look over his shoulder in the direction the elder gazed. As promised, Vaspara was striding toward them. From what he could tell over the distance, she was fully recovered, almost glowing with new life.

Dressed in full armor, she was a sight to inspire fear in a mortal.

Good thing he wasn't mortal.

Vaspara had a word with Mattis, and then the elder nodded and headed off to attend to whatever errand she'd asked of him.

"You look better. Good." Vaspara's statement lacked any kind of warmth. "We need to discuss plans. We can't stay this close to the Battle Goddess's kingdom. As soon as you're flight worthy again, we need to scout for a place to settle, even if it's just temporary."

He had expected nothing romantic to come out of Vaspara's mouth, since their situation was precarious. Talk about their relationship would have to wait. "The farther away, the better. Perhaps even another world, once the war is over. If we try to perform a great weaving now, the Battle Goddess will sense it and send hunters after us. But if we hide somewhere on this world, perhaps near one of our less lethal enemies and don't call upon any great drawings of power, we should be able to remain invisible until after the war has decimated both armies."

Vaspara made a sound of agreement. "Afterward, all three realms will be a safer place for a while."

"Yes. While I expect the Lord of the Underworld to win this war, the price will be high. His gargoyle army will be greatly depleted and take eons to rebuild. In the meantime, we should be able to live in relative peace if we can get far enough away from the Battle Goddess's kingdom."

Pacing in a half circle, she came to a stop next to him and leaned a hip against a tree trunk. "I think we must find our new home and take the servants there before we double back to rescue your brood. Once we rescue them, we won't have time to dally and hunt for a place to hole up."

As much as his instincts were telling him to rush back and collect his eggs, that would be a poorly thought out plan. It was doubtful the Battle Goddess would even think about his nest, having greater concerns to deal with after the most recent raid gone bad. His clutch should be safe where they were for now. At least for a little while. "I'll begin the hunt this afternoon."

"You should wait a day. Rest. You can't be fully recovered yet." Concern entered her voice and little wrinkles formed around her eyes.

"It barely even aches." He stomped the ground to prove his point. "It won't affect my speed. Plus, with the dense tree cover, there won't be any running. Once I reach the ocean, I'll wait for night and take to the air once I've scouted the area to be certain no one is near enough to see me. Discovery is our greatest danger."

"I'm coming with you in case you run into a scout. If

there is a fight, the two of us will have a better chance of killing him or her before they can get out a warning."

"I concur." Sorac fought back a grin. It would likely take days to find a suitable, uninhabited island somewhere out in the ocean. If there were no other males available, she'd turn to him for another feeding. Again, it might not lead to romance, but he wouldn't find providing what she needed a chore either.

Eventually, he'd win over the succubus and convince her to be the mother to his brood.

"Fine. We'll leave as soon as I gather supplies."

"How are our servants for food?" Sorac asked. "I'll hunt them up fresh meat before we leave if needed."

"Mattis says the valley is rich in game and an abundance of berry bushes grow along the river. They've already gathered a good stockpile of supplies for the winter. We can take some of that with us and then later help with the hunting and gathering to increase the winter stores."

Sorac shuddered at the mention of winter. He hated winter. Firedrakes loved heat. The hotter, the better. "Maybe we should scout in a southernly direction first. We might luck out and find an island chain rich in plant and animal life."

Vaspara grinned at him. "I think I detect an ulterior motive that involves warm sands."

He shrugged. "That is a possibility."

CHAPTER SIX

The scouting expedition took longer than Vaspara thought it would. Sorac headed south immediately, his massive wings eating up the distance. Three days later, they were in much warmer climates.

That was the easy part.

Finding an island that didn't already have nesting fire-drakes was more difficult.

While Sorac was big and powerful, and Vaspara could easily handle herself in a magical fight, they needed to avoid significant expenditures of magic, or they risked drawing unwanted attention. Since giving up was not an option, they continued south and east without complaint. On their ninth day of travel, they spotted a likely-looking island.

"That looks promising," Vaspara said as she took in the sight of the island in the distance. "I see no flying fire-drakes, and we must almost be on the opposite side of the planet from the Lord of the Underworld's island and far south of the Battle Goddess's kingdom."

"This might be it." He agreed as he winged his way closer.

As much as she enjoyed flying with the big drake, she was also looking forward to exploring the island on foot. She missed Sorac in his man form. Though, she admitted with chagrin, that might be because it had been three days since she last fed and even after only two feedings, she'd developed quite the taste for his magical essence.

And he was plenty skilled enough to leave her physically satisfied and magically replenished. Sorac, too, had grown in strength after each feeding.

He drifted lower and circled the island, seeking signs of docks or boats or other large predators. When they spotted nothing more dangerous than a few large cats and a host of snakes, Sorac winged his way deeper into the island.

"That peak," Vaspara pointed. "It looks like an extinct volcano."

"It does." He changed direction in the air and darted toward the volcanic mountain with its softly rounded peaks and mantle of greenery. There was a lake in the center.

"The walls might provide natural protection against the powerful winds of tropical storms."

"We could carve out dwellings in the walls and reinforce them with magic," Sorac said, warming to the idea.

"And if that monster," Vaspara pointed at the dormant volcano, "ever wakes up, you'd warn us, right? I'm not such a lover of heat as you are."

Sorac laughed. "Yes, I would sense its waking months in advance. We can even build a second village at the opposite end of the island as a precaution. Two homes. One here, for the storm season, another along the ocean for the calm time when we'll do most of our fishing, hunting, and gathering."

Vaspara stroked a hand down his smooth, warm scales. "Thank you for finding this place. I think we can make a home here."

"As do I," he agreed. "Shall I land so we can look around?"

"Yes," Vaspara called out, her voice ringing with foreign joy.

It had been so long since she'd felt true happiness, she almost didn't recognize the sensation bubbling up inside her.

Sorac came in for a landing along the beach. Once on the ground, Vaspara removed the travel bags from his harness and then slid down from the firedrake's high back to land in the sand. She immediately knew she was overdressed for the heat. Even the ocean breeze felt warm here at sea level. It would take some getting used to, she supposed, but it was better than facing yet another pointless war.

Pulling out a waterskin from one pack, she took a long drink before glancing over at Sorac. He'd wandered a short distance away and was pawing at the sand. A moment later he circled and before she could shout for him to stop, he flopped down on his belly, kicking and twisting and rolling in delight.

Waves of sand flew in all directions. Including at her, coating her skin and hair. It quickly found its way into every gap in her armor and under her clothing.

"Damn it, Lizardman! Stop that."

The waves of sand stopped flying and a deep rumbling apology vibrated in the air just above her head.

"Sorry. I couldn't resist."

Vaspara continued to spit sand and then carefully shook her hair, keeping her eyes scrunched tightly shut to save them from getting scoured with sand like the rest of her body. "Damn sand will be gritting between my teeth for the next moon cycle."

"Rinse your mouth with water," he added helpfully.

She kicked sand at his face. It didn't get into his eyes; the tiny grains just rolled off his scales.

With an altogether too happy sounding grunt, he rolled on his back, presenting his underbelly to the sky, head upside down. He just lay like that, looking like a silly ass.

Vaspara said as much, and the firedrake grinned, steam and little flicks of fire seeping from between his sharp teeth. She scowled back at him, trying her damnedest not to laugh.

Eventually, she admitted defeat and chuckled at his antics. Deciding a swim to cool off sounded like a delightful idea, she walked toward the water's edge, unbuckling and discarding her armor as she moved. Her boots were next to go, followed by her leather pants and vest. She pulled her shirt over her head and dropped it on the ground. Next, she shoved her undergarments down, and then walked naked along the shoreline, letting the waves wash over her feet.

She couldn't remember ever feeling so free.

Sorac had stopped rolling, his gaze locked on her instead. She ran her eyes over him and smirked.

"I'm going for a swim. You're welcome to come, too. But if you want me to help you do something about that extra leg you're sporting, better shift back to a man first. I might be a succubus, but even we have limitations."

Not waiting for a reply, she continued in a jaunty little walk that would jiggle certain body parts enough to stop most males in their tracks. Sorac was far from indifferent to her charms.

Besides, she thought to herself with a little smile, *I am overdue for a good feeding.*

By the sound of the big splash, the firedrake had darted into the water.

She was forging her way into deeper water by the time Sorac, now wearing his man form, joined her.

"Someone is eager," she said breezily, even though she was feeling the exact same.

"Always." Sorac took her in his arms and kissed her shoulder.

The sun had sunk below the horizon quite some time ago and the first moon to rise was already making its way across a field of stars. The second would rise soon, and

Sorac should likely be sleeping, but his mind refused to rest.

Which was strange. Vaspara had relaxed his body enough that wakefulness shouldn't be a problem. But instead, he was staring up at the sky, dreaming about a future Vaspara hadn't agreed to yet.

Even after he rescued his brood, they still wouldn't hatch until they sensed the presence of two adults ready and willing to rear them. It was a firedrake survival trait, since it took two parents to share the required magic the young drakelings would need growing up.

Vaspara enjoyed his body. She made no secret of that, and she loved him, had admitted that, but she still hadn't said she wanted to advance their relationship. Actually, he was rather confident the thought of helping to raise his little ones terrified the succubus.

"How do I make you want me for more than my body?" Sorac whispered softly to a sleeping Vaspara.

At the sound of his voice, she snuggled close and crooned something against his shoulder. Grinning, he realized perhaps she already wanted far more than his body. As for his clutch, maybe all he needed to do was place one egg in Vaspara's arms and wait for the little one to sing to her.

Grinning, Sorac pulled his lovely succubus closer to his side and watched the stars spin across the sky.

Yes, he thought in the moments before his mind surrendered to sleep, *this island will be a good place for Vaspara and me to raise our family.*

CHAPTER SEVEN

The island paradise seemed like a dream though really it had only been a handful of days since they'd left their new home to return to the valley where they'd stashed their servants. The wind off the mountains felt cold enough to chill her soul. Or perhaps that was caused by looking upon the Battle Goddess's fortress again.

That also seemed like something from another life.

Have I changed so much in so short of time? she wondered. *Or was the chill caused by fear? Fear of what would happen to her dreams if she and Sorac were caught sneaking into the fortress.*

"We need a plan in case they catch us," Sorac said, echoing her thoughts so closely she wondered if she'd let down her shields and invited him into her mind without even realizing it.

Vaspara glanced from him and then back to the black stone of the fortress. "Actually, I think I might have a plan. If we get caught, we can claim we believe there's a traitor in the fortress and that unknown person informed Lord Death of our coming. We're just sneaking in to keep the rumor of our demise circulating so we can hunt the traitor without them growing suspicious."

His teeth flashed white in the darkness. "I like the plan. It's partly true. There will be traitors within once we enter."

"Lies are always easier when they're partly true," Vaspara agreed.

"Who do we hate enough to claim is the traitor? The Battle Goddess might torture them before she realizes we lied to escape with my brood."

Grinning, Vaspara crawled higher up the slope so she could better visually scout the terrain below them for patrols. "Honestly, I don't care which captain we finger as long as it isn't Bervicta. The others are either cruel, ambitious, or as likely to stab someone in the back as hold a conversation with them."

"How about the first one we see who isn't Bervicta then?"

Vaspara shrugged. "Works for me."

"Good. It's settled then. Let's go collect my brood."

Nodding her agreement, she started back down the hill they'd crawled up to study the activity at the front gate. There was no way to sneak in through one of the gates, but they were both long-serving captains and knew of other ways into the well-guarded structure.

Vaspara followed Sorac as he made his way down the spillway. The underground tunnels were dark, but at least they were dry, no storm had dumped rain on the mountains for a few days. As a half-succubus, she could see in the dark with no trouble and Sorac's firedrake heritage gifted him with the ability to see variances in temperature. He'd said firedrakes had developed that ability to aid them in hunting prey and judging thermal currents in the air during flight.

Navigating the darkened tunnels was relatively easy. So was dispatching the four guards on duty at the entrance of the tunnels. Between them, they had rendered the soldiers unconscious without alerting the rest of the keep. Killing them would have been even faster, but these were warriors she and Sorac had trained.

They couldn't just kill them because it would make their own lives easier.

But after that first hurdle, the rest of the tunnels were empty. Since they had waited until just after shift change, they had many hours to get in, pack the eggs in the travel bags, and then make their escape.

They would be long gone before the guards at the tunnel's entrance regained consciousness.

The journey up didn't take long. Soon they emerged into a spacious chamber. It was dark except for the soft glow of the dome spell surrounding the nest. Beyond the transparent shimmer, Vaspara could make out the slightly pointed top of each egg.

"Is the dome going to be a problem?" Vaspara asked as

she circled the stone ring around the nest, hunting for other traps.

"No," Sorac said as he joined her. "The dome is mine. I sense no other magic upon it or near it."

He reached out and touched the dome. Lines of glowing power appeared, and Sorac chanted softly as he drew a counterspell. With a shiver and a burst of light, the top of the dome folded down upon itself until it vanished into bright runes carved into the stone floor.

Vaspara had her first clear look at the fourteen eggs, each one about the length between her wrist and elbow. Years ago, she'd seen one of his eggs when Brakaya brought it to her. That one had been a pale green with darker diamond shape markings. Two of the other eggs shared a similar color and pattern, but the rest ranged from blue to dark reddish purple.

She hadn't expected them to be so pretty, but then again, firedrakes came in a myriad of jewel tones.

"The colors of the shells reflect the shade the drakelings will turn upon reaching maturity. They'll all be a muddy olive green at first."

"How did you discover that bit about the colors?"

"Like everything else. I asked the herb witches or read it in an ancient book or scroll." He shrugged. "So far, everything has proven correct. I imagine this will as well."

"The herb witches are correct. I wonder how many died to gather that information?" The new voice came from somewhere in the darkness to the left of the nest. "If given a chance, your offspring will grow into prime specimens."

Vaspara turned to face the unseen threat, her sword already naked in her hand. Strangely, her sight couldn't pierce the darkness. There wasn't much besides a gargoyle that could hide from her, and she was sure no gargoyles hid within these walls.

"Who's there?" Sorac growled in threat.

His power spiked enough Vaspara could feel its heat against her skin, although, he hadn't shifted forms yet. Shifting would prevent a quick escape through tunnels too small for his large firedrake form.

A rippling stirred the air and unexpected color and light spilled into the chamber as a fissure split the air and darkness. A being of pure power took several strides into the room and halted. His shimmering, power-shrouded form dimmed enough Vaspara could see him a little more clearly.

Veins and coils of magic whipped around his form before slowly being absorbed back into his body. After a moment, the lines of burning power shifted, becoming tattoos that covered much of his bronze-toned skin. Even as his body took on a more mortal appearance, his eyes still glowed like two pools of molten lava.

The tattoos, brightening and dimming as if someone was blowing upon hot coals, making them glow brighter by turns, were mesmerizing. Unlike his tattoos, his burning gaze maintained the same steady intensity as he regarded them.

This male was beautiful, in a terrifying sort of way. His shape and form designed to appeal to men and women alike. That was the great jest, wasn't it? Everything about him was a carefully constructed deception, a lie to capture or stun the unwary, to blind them while he worked to free himself and destroy everything around him.

A djinn.

They'd stumbled into a djinn-designed trap.

Of course. He was the one creature that could have seen the outcome of the battle without even being present. It was the nature of a djinn to know things. It was partly why they were such deadly opponents.

He tilted his head as he studied first Sorac, then her, and at last the fourteen eggs. His next move surprised her.

Grasping his hands behind his back, he walked a large circle around them instead of attacking as she'd expected. His long strides made the glowing power swathing his lower body ripple and dance like flames in a breeze. When he was still again, the power calmed, settling around him like a skirt.

As she watched, his body grew more substantial, and greater details showed. She scanned for weapons. He was naked from the waist up, and a wide belt and the skirt-like power shimmering around his legs seemed the only items he wore. And even those were likely just a manifestation of his power.

She saw no weapons.

But then again, he needed none. He was the weapon.

A weapon placed here to capture or kill them. Vaspara felt despair. Never again would she see that perfect island or get to live out her foolish dream of a quiet, peaceful life. Why had she thought it was possible? The Divine Ones hated ones such as her and Sorac.

And here, now, was their deaths come to meet them.

Neither of them could beat a djinn, not by themselves. Perhaps if they led their battalions, they could trap or destroy the djinn before it could wipe them all from existence. But here, alone, only the two of them?

Vaspara knew defeat when she saw it. "Kill us and make it quick. Our torture will bring you no benefit or honor."

'Divine Ones,' Vaspara sent up a very rare prayer, *'if you have even a little mercy in your hearts for ones born of darkness, you will kill Sorac before you kill me or his brood. Let him die attempting to protect those he loves at least. Don't make him watch.'*

The djinn laughed. "Firedrake, you picked a considerate partner. She'll make you a worthy mate."

Vaspara and Sorac glanced at each other.

What did the djinn care? He was playing games, obviously, though she didn't know why. Neither of them had command of the bottle used to trap him. Playing with them wouldn't free the creature.

Perhaps he was bored—a terrible thought.

"I am not here at the behest of my master to kill you." With a ripple of power and graceful muscles, the djinn moved closer. "I never even told her you were both alive."

"Why?" Vaspara might be stepping squarely in his trap, but she was curious, and nothing she did at this point could do anything to sway the djinn.

"They never thought to ask me. And as I would get no benefit, there was no point in me sharing the information."

"What do you want then?"

"My freedom."

CHAPTER EIGHT

"Take me with you. Free me from this place. If you do this for me, I shall allow you to collect your eggs, and we can then all leave this place." The djinn waved a hand and a new dome formed over the nest.

Vaspara knew this one wouldn't answer to anyone except the djinn.

"How are you able to call magic without a command?"

"I was given some leniency for the defense of this kingdom."

Sorac shifted his weight, taking on a better fighting stance. Vaspara realized she'd done the same.

"Be at ease. Since the Battle Goddess hasn't yet stripped you of your ranks, you are both still captains, and off limits to me. There is also nothing in my orders that demands I act in this case." He gave them a sardonic smile. "Mortals truly should not play with djinn."

No, Vaspara agreed. They should not.

"Aid me, and we can all leave this place before the Battle Goddess and my blood witch mistress," he practically chewed the last word before spitting it out, "is aware I'm gone. If you do not aid me, then I shall report you to the witch."

Vaspara narrowed her eyes. She knew a thing or two about djinn. Something didn't add up. "You hate her. Anyone with eyes can see that. Why would you aid her?"

"She grants me the freedom to explore the fortress for short times." He grinned wickedly. "A reward for good behavior."

Good behavior? Not likely.

Unlike when they were in the Spirit Realm, once a djinn was stolen from that place, they turned dark and destructive, filled with rage for the divinity they'd lost. Their one drive was to return to the Spirit Realm at any cost.

Djinns had been known to destroy entire continents as they made their escape back to their home realm or perished in the attempt.

The djinn's statement likely meant he'd already begun to influence and perhaps even exert control over Taryin. With a djinn, if a master weren't careful, they'd swiftly become the slave without ever realizing it.

"Will you aid me, or shall I drag you before the Lady of Battles? She'll be glad to see you both, I'm sure. Perhaps I'll earn some other reward?"

She and Sorac glanced sidelong at each other. They were both aware of the deadly nature of a djinn, but also that they had no choice but to bring this one with them if they wanted to escape. Vaspara nodded ever so slightly.

"We'll bring you with us," Sorac agreed.

"Where is your bottle?" Vaspara added, knowing wherever it was, it wouldn't be easy to reach.

The djinn tilted his head toward her. "The Lady of Battles placed the vessel between the four anchors that lock her chains to this temple."

Sorac cursed. "She wants you to escape your enslavement and return to the Spirit Realm, destroying the spell the Avatars created that traps her here when you go."

"Yes," the djinn purred.

Vaspara swallowed against the nervousness tightening her throat. "She thinks she'll survive, but this place, and everyone within it, will be destroyed."

"Yes, as a failsafe should she lose the war. She doesn't want to remain imprisoned here for thousands of years more. My power, once unleashed, will react with the Avatars' ancient spell and together it will be enough to destroy this world, ensuring the Battle Goddess's freedom."

Sorac glanced at Vaspara again, his expression saying he thought this djinn was being abnormally talkative. She concurred.

"For some reason you don't want to cause that destruction," Vaspara mused. "I don't know why you'd care. Everything we know about your kind says you are heartless in your drive to return to the Spirit Realm. You aren't supposed to care how many you kill."

The djinn laughed, the cruel sound sending a chill down

her spine. "You and every other mortal might think I'm a monster, but I am not. Not yet. I do not want to undo a spell that cost the Avatars so much to create."

Vaspara noted his comment made no mention of preventing the death of millions.

He turned from them to approach the eggs, his living, ember-like tattoos flaring brightly against his dark skin. He stared down at the eggs for a long moment. Vaspara didn't dare move a muscle.

Thank the Divine Ones the firedrake kept his instincts in check. It couldn't have been easy with a djinn admiring his nest.

"I was there," the djinn said at last. "I watched the creation of the duality curse that binds the twins. And, later, I nursed the one you know as the Avatars. Weakened by giving everything of itself, the Avatar damaged its soul and could not blend itself back into one being as it always did upon returning to the Spirit Realm. It took a very long time for my siblings and me to restore the two halves of the sundered soul."

"I understand why you want to get away," Vaspara whispered.

"No, you don't. But one day you will know what it is like to watch helplessly as the one you love is hurting. I do not wish to be the one to cause my oldest companion such hurt. I must get far from this place before I break free of this vessel prison. So, you will take me with you when you leave, and once the Avatars return to this realm to face the Lady of Battles, you will take my bottle to them, and they will find a way to free me without destroying this world."

There was something the djinn wasn't telling them. Vaspara had spent a lifetime learning to read people. Knowing who could be trusted and who would try to kill her to achieve their own ambitions was something she'd had to perfect. Her survival depended upon it.

And this djinn was holding something back.

"What aren't you telling me?"

"The one who summoned and trapped me is stronger than any blood witch to ever plague the universe before. Worse, the Battle Goddess has been teaching her things to which no agent of darkness should be privy." The djinn turned back to Vaspara, a grimace just vanishing from his features. "She found a way to do more than enslave a djinn. Her power is infusing me with her taint. If I can't get free of her soon, I'll become more of a monster than you can ever envision."

Cold sweat dripped down Vaspara's back, but she knew what had to be done. Some things transcended concepts of good and evil. This was one. The djinn had to be taken from this place and somehow returned to the Avatars. There was no option for failure. They could work out the 'how' later. "We will steal the vessel that traps you and then we'll make our escape."

"Your oath that you will take me to the Avatars," the djinn said, hissing some words as his magic flared in warning.

Vaspara fisted her hand and thumped it against her chest. "On my honor and my life, I will do all in my power to get you safely away from the Battle Goddess's territory."

Sorac mimicked Vaspara's gesture and oath. "Although,

with the Avatars in the Mortal Realm, there's the problem of how to reach them. Neither Vaspara nor I have the magical strength or knowledge to create a portal spell to travel there."

"A hurdle to overcome at another time," the djinn said.

CHAPTER NINE

After the djinn had acquired their agreement, he'd vanished, returning to his vessel to await them, he claimed. With his departure, Vaspara relaxed only a little. She and Sorac continued on foot, ghosting down little-used corridors until they reached a wider tunnel.

Here, they were careful to pick their way over and around the four lengths of glowing chains that stretched off in both directions. The slightest touch of the chains would be enough to maim or kill even someone as strong as Sorac. The flare of magic would also alert the Battle Goddess that someone was down here. She'd then rush to capture or kill the intruder.

The chains had been known to punish the Lady of Battles even if she wasn't the one tampering with them. At least they weren't shifting and slithering. The demigoddess must be at rest. There was no telling how long that would last.

She and Sorac hurried as much as they could before the chains changed from an annoyance into something much deadlier and harder to avoid.

Their destination wasn't far. With luck, they would get in, get the djinn's bottle, and get out all without ever having to look upon the demigoddess again.

"Divine Ones be merciful," Vaspara muttered.

Not that they ever were to ones such as she and Sorac.

She was just stepping over a chain when it shifted suddenly as the Battle Goddess moved somewhere in the levels above. Vaspara leaped over one chain, and only narrowly missed brushing against another link.

Cursing softly, she danced over and around them as links slithered on up the tunnel. The thigh-high links weren't the easiest things to jump when they weren't moving. Behind her Sorac cursed.

"You all right?" she called softly when the chains were still again.

"Yes, one of them nearly brushed my scabbard. Should have left it behind."

Vaspara realized he was correct and swiftly unbuckled hers, holding it in her hands instead. Picking their careful way along, they were soon having to weave, dart, and leap over the links as they moved again.

"Curse it. She must be pacing."

Sorac snorted. "Probably worrying over how she will ever find worthy replacements for us."

"I might find that funnier if we weren't risking our lives for the djinn."

At last, the Battle Goddess stopped moving, and the chains stilled.

Vaspara glanced over her shoulder at Sorac. They were both panting. "This would have made a good captains' test. Too bad we never thought of it."

He grinned. "Yes, it would, wouldn't it?"

They came to the end of the tunnel. It was much lighter here; the glow bleeding off the anchors was stronger than the chains themselves. She shielded her eyes while they adjusted to the brighter environment.

"Here," Sorac called as he circled around the glowing crystal pillars growing out of the bedrock. "I found the djinn's bottle."

Vaspara joined him once she could see again. It looked like someone had set the bottle in the central space between each of the fiery pillars, just dropped there like a bit of trash.

"Do you sense any spells?" she asked. "I can't, not over the power those things are giving off." She gestured at the anchor pillars.

"No. Nothing. I doubt any other spells could survive here."

"There are no spells of protection because there was no need," the djinn said as he appeared behind them.

Vaspara spun to face the djinn, still not trusting him.

"The blood witch and the demigoddess assume no one is foolish enough to venture into her territory without her knowing, certainly not to come down here and risk their souls." The djinn grinned. "But these are interesting times, and neither of them are parents. They didn't factor in what two parents will do for their young."

"I'm not a parent," Vaspara groused.

"Not yet, but you will make the fiercest of mothers."

She didn't bother to respond, instead moving closer to the pillars. "I'm narrower through the shoulders," she told Sorac, "I'll get the djinn's bottle. Just steady my hips and legs and make sure they don't brush the pillars or the chains. And for the love of your eggs, grab me if the demigoddess moves again."

Sorac stepped in behind her and took hold of her belt to quickly pull her out from between the pillars if need be. Once she was between them, he switched his hold to her hips and slowly slid her forward.

Vaspara took in every detail around her, ready to react to the tiniest shimmy in the chains. But they remained still as she stretched until her fingers closed around the pretty little bottle. "Got it. Pull me out."

Sorac did, and then they both stood there for long moments and stared down at the bottle.

"Tuck that someplace safe," the djinn ordered, "and let us leave this place. We've been lucky so far. Blood Witch Taryin hasn't called on me to aid in spell work yet tonight, but she will. Best I am too far away to react to her summons."

Vaspara nodded and swiftly tucked the jar into the padded bag slung across her shoulder. All the others were back in the underground egg chamber.

Once the bottle was safely stored, she looked up at the two males. "Let's go."

CHAPTER TEN

Sorac didn't relax until they were back in the chamber housing his eggs. He hadn't liked a moment of the time Vaspara was belly down between the crystalline pillars, with their piles of coiled chains that could move at any moment.

If the Battle Goddess had descended deeper within her temple, the chains would have retracted themselves, narrowing the space between each of the pillars. It had been a tense few moments while Vaspara had been vulnerable.

But it pleased him she trusted him with her life.

Now they were back with his eggs, still not out of danger by any stretch, but soon.

He glanced over his shoulder at the djinn. "We've done our part. Time to hold up your end of the bargain."

Sorac jerked his chin at the eggs.

"Once given, I honor my word." The djinn waved one hand almost dismissively at the shield, and it shimmered more brightly for a moment before vanishing into the bedrock as Sorac's own spell had done earlier.

"I shall return to my vessel until after your escape. I'm much less noticeable that way."

The djinn chuckled in amusement, but even that he managed to make chilling, Sorac mused as he gently lifted an egg and placed it in the individual padded sections Alaya had sewn into each bag to keep the eggs from bumping together during flight. Beside him, Vaspara picked up the first egg. He could see that its weight and heat surprised her.

"They're warm. You can feel their souls," she said, her surprise evident.

"Of course," Sorac said as he gathered up the next one.

Not having been around many infants or eggs, he realized Vaspara probably hadn't expected the sparks of life to already be so powerful.

She was even more careful picking up the next one. When she held it at arm's length until she wrestled the bag open, he grinned again. It was clear she was afraid of accidentally banging the satchel against the nest's stone rim.

"I don't think I've ever seen you look so flustered," Sorac added with a grin. Seeing this new side of Vaspara made warmth curl in his belly, and then his loins. "They're eggs, not deadly weapons intent upon destroying you."

Vaspara flashed her fangs at him. "I'm more afraid of me destroying them than the other way around."

"You're doing fine."

That only made Vaspara flush a darker red. She filled the next bag in silence as they worked swiftly. Soon all fourteen eggs were in the seven bags. Sorac carried four but allowed her to take the other three. It was important Vaspara knew he trusted her with his brood.

"Let's hope we don't have to fight our way out."

"No," he agreed, the thought an ominous one.

They were lucky and made it out of the tunnel system and back into the wild lands beyond the fortress without incident.

Vaspara stopped to survey the area and then muttered something under her breath.

"Sorry. I didn't catch that."

Glancing sidelong at him, she laughed. "I was just thanking the Divine Ones for taking pity on fourteen innocent lives."

As soon as she said it, she glanced down at one of the travel bags, the one with its cargo of two eggs and one djinn hiding in his bottle. "Or perhaps the Divine Ones had a secondary motive. It wouldn't surprise me if they wanted the djinn far away from the Lady of Battles and they used us to accomplish that feat. Whatever the case, we made it out of the fortress."

Sorac grunted in agreement. "Now we have to avoid all patrols, and then we can begin our new life with our drakelings."

Vaspara didn't correct him. He hoped that meant she was warming to the idea of their new family.

They kept up a brisk walk for the rest of the night. By midmorning, Sorac deemed they were far enough away he could shift back to his firedrake form without the flare of magic giving their position away. Once in his true form, he paused long enough for Vaspara to harness him, tie on his precious cargo, and settle herself on his back.

He wasn't at all concerned with being spotted. Firedrakes were masters of camouflage, able to take on the colors of their surroundings.

When they reached the valley, the two human families had everything packed and ready to strap onto his harness. Once the supplies were in place, Mattis oversaw the others as they settled between Sorac's tall spine ridges and locked themselves in place with straps across their thighs.

The added weight of all the supplies plus his human and succubus cargo would slow him, but only a little.

Soon, loaded like a pack animal, he set off on foot again.

Once they made it to the ocean with no sign of pursuit, he stopped long enough for everyone to stretch their legs and relieve themselves before climbing back aboard. Soon enough, he was winging his way out over the ocean.

As a precaution, he flew northwest for most of the first day before turning and heading south at last. The blood witch and the Battle Goddess would know the djinn was missing by now. If they sent scouts, he wanted none of the fishermen from the surrounding villages to tell them they'd seen a firedrake winging his way south.

Heading north and west would delay and confuse any followers long enough they'd never track him down even if the Battle Goddess sent a company of harpies after them.

Sorac stopped a few times each day to give his passengers and himself a chance to rest and check on the eggs and the djinn. Soon everyone fell into a routine. Though there was nothing he could do to protect his riders from the elements, and they found their skin burned and chapped from the sun and the wind.

At least, he avoided storms by skirting around them.

The djinn didn't appear from his bottle until the third day of travel to the south. He didn't need rest, food, or drink, but he seemed to enjoy walking the beaches of each island they stopped at, searching out many kinds of plant and animal life to admire.

"They are all so different when they are just souls in the Spirit Realm," he said once in passing.

Vaspara and Sorac exchanged a look but merely nodded as if they understood. But Sorac doubted anyone living in the magic or mortal realms could truly understand the mind of a djinn. At least, no one besides the Avatars. Perhaps the Sorceress and the Gargoyle Protector could understand how this creature's mind worked just fine.

For their part, the servants steered well clear of the djinn, and he seemed to ignore them, which Sorac decided was good for the mortals.

On another one of their stops, Sorac, Vaspara, and the djinn sat around a bonfire and watched the ocean. After several days' travel, Sorac had begun to relax around the djinn. As far as big scary things went, he'd travel with the spirit creature any day over the blood witch.

Sipping at his tea—which was just water with some herbs sprinkled over the top—Sorac eyed the djinn. "I'm not naïve enough to ask for your name and expect an answer, but surely you must be getting tired of being called Djinn. How would you like to be addressed?"

"Djinn is fine."

Well, so much for that, Sorac mused.

Soon the conversation turned to talk about how they would return the djinn to the Avatars.

"Our best bet might be attempting to speak with Gryton, since they rescued him," Sorac offered.

"If he's still alive," Vaspara countered. "We don't even know why they rescued him. Perhaps they saw it as an opportunity to grab one of the inner circle and learn what the Battle Goddess has been up to these last few years."

The djinn tilted his head one way and then another. "You mean you don't know what Gryton is?"

"No," Sorac injected and then glanced at Vaspara. Neither of the ex-captains said anything more, fearing to interrupt the djinn.

The djinn glanced up from studying the bonfire. "He is their son. The first being created between them without divine will driving them."

Their son. The Avatars had broken their most sacred law and begotten a child. Sorac swore his mind stalled for a moment. Gods, Gryton was their son.

Clearing his throat, he met the djinn's eyes. "I do not doubt your words, but this will take some getting used to."

Sorac had always known there was something more to Gryton. He just hadn't realized it was... this.

"I can't believe we never knew," Vaspara just shook her head in disbelief, "And that he didn't tell us."

"He trusted no one. Not even us. Not really. Otherwise, he would have enlisted us to help with Anna and Shadowlight's escape." Together the three of them would have been strong enough to kill Blood Witch Taryin and blame her death on Anna and the cub during the escape.

"Gryton's parentage changes nothing. We still must hide until the Avatars come to this realm," the djinn said, sounding unhappy but resigned about that fate.

"Well," Vaspara said from where she was stretched out next to the fire, looking up at the sky. "That complicates things more than a little? Still, I'd take Gryton and the Avatars' side over that of the blood witch."

"Let's hope someone gives us that choice." The djinn gazed up at the sky, studying the same stars Vaspara had been a moment ago.

Having to guard this being from the Spirit Realm would be interesting, and perhaps harrowing. Sorac just hoped the Avatars didn't kill either of the Battle Goddess's ex-captains when they held up their end of the bargain and gave the djinn and his bottle into their keeping.

He wanted to live to raise his little ones with a certain succubus now that he'd finally started to soften her to the idea.

Long after Vaspara had fallen asleep, and the djinn had returned to his bottle, Sorac turned his gaze up to the heavens.

"I know we didn't start out on the best of terms, but I will serve you now if you'll have me."

If the Divine Ones responded, it was lost in the sound of the surf and the ocean breeze.

CHAPTER ELEVEN

As it turned out, their island home took shape faster than Vaspara thought possible. Oh, there was a great deal they didn't have, but with Sorac's help, they could make saws, axes, and other basic farming implements.

A firedrake's ability to breathe fire was a great weapon on the battlefield, but here in their new village, Vaspara got to see another side. Sorac had an uncanny ability to sniff out veins of metal buried in the earth.

He took the better part of a day to map the best places to dig for various metals, but once he'd picked out the choicest spots, he utilized his considerable strength, stamina, and sharp claws to dig out the ore.

His fiery breath allowed him to melt and refine the ore until it was ready to be poured into molds for various tools they could use for building and farming. He even took the time to forge a massive plow and harrow he could drag behind him in firedrake form to work the land.

Seed they would collect from nature for now, but eventually they'd need to approach other kingdoms and trade.

"You've been thinking about this for a long time, haven't you?" Vaspara challenged as she looked at one of his drawings of the harrow. "How else do you even know how to build one of these?"

Sorac grimaced. "It was more of a fantasy than a realistic dream, but I knew one day I wanted a place to nest and raise my clutch. From that dream, I spun a few other, more elaborate, dreams. In my spare time, I studied what the villagers and farmers did to work the land and grow crops. I also studied textiles and how to cure a hide."

Vaspara frowned.

"What's wrong?"

"I don't know how to do any of that," she admitted. "I hate being useless and ignorant."

"You, my lovely succubus, are neither of those things."

She planted her fist on her hips. "I'm good at building defenses, killing things, and planning how to kill things."

Sorac laughed. "You are very good at sex, too."

She rolled her eyes. "That doesn't make me feel any better, you great lizard."

"Forgive me. My humor sometimes misses the mark."

"Of course it does. You're male."

"Lucky for you," he countered with a wiggle of one brow before turning serious once more. "You are far more valuable than just what you can do. But if it makes you feel better, I could teach you. Besides, I could use help with this task."

Vaspara jumped at the chance to learn and feel like she was contributing something more valuable than just hunting and gathering.

Over the next two moon cycles, she found she was good at making the tools, especially axes or anything with a sharp edge.

After all, they were a little like weapons, just ones used to slay trees and other plants. Soon she was creating better designs than Sorac's originals, her tactician's mind able to see patterns and apply them to parchment and then turn them into usable tools with the firedrake's help.

When Sorac wasn't busy with that, he was spending all his free time at his temporary nest with his clutch. The nest was in the center of the area that would eventually be a village. They'd laid it out a little inland from the spot in the harbor where they'd planned to later build docks for fishing boats.

She'd soon learned boats were another of the firedrake's hobbies. Who would have thought something that floated upon the water would fascinate a winged creature?

But it was another benefit they'd use one day. The first priorities were the village and Sorac's permanent nest. For his nest, he'd picked a high point east of where they were building the village. Digging away the soft dirt until he'd reached the volcanic rock below, he created a shallow depression and carried sand from the beach to line the entire area.

Once that was done, he'd taken his eggs and moved them to this new location, where he'd arranged them in the sand, fussing until he had everything perfect. He kept the djinn's bottle close to the eggs, using the magic that bled off the bottle naturally as extra food for the developing clutch.

That first day, as Vaspara had watched, he'd circled the eggs several times before lying down and mantling his wings over them. When he'd blasted them with his fiery breath, heating the layer of sand until it formed glass, Vaspara had bolted upright in surprise.

But the eggs were those of a firedrake, and they grew stronger each time he blew fire across their shells, he explained. He was a diligent parent, carefully turning each egg so it wouldn't become locked into the sand-turned-to-glass footing of the nest.

In between the hot firings, he would croon to them, a beautiful song that filled the surrounding area.

Today, she assumed Sorac was with his clutch again since she hadn't seen him down at the village area. She'd been so busy with the village construction, where she'd been helping to build houses, Vaspara hadn't had time to seek out Sorac for more than a quick word or two in more than four days.

She missed their chats where they used to talk of inane things after a long day of training soldiers and new recruits.

That was how she found herself approaching his nest again with its waist-high, thick glass sides. Sorac wasn't here, she noted. Hmm, he must be down at the beach gathering more sand to line the nest.

Ah, well, she thought with a surprising twinge of relief, *I can always come back later.*

It took her a moment to realize the reason for the relief. When she looked back over the last few days, she came to understand she'd been using the excuse of being busy to avoid Sorac when he was at his nest. She was aware how desperately he wanted her to be his brood's mother figure, and that frightened her.

"When did I become such a coward? That stops now," she muttered aloud. With a frown, she circled the nest, walked to a fallen log, and sat to await Sorac's return.

Is what Sorac wants so terrible?

No, she decided. Not for her, but perhaps it would be for the drakelings.

It wasn't like a half-demon succubus would make a good mother. She lacked the barest instinct to guide her.

But hadn't she known nothing about creating tools, building houses, and farming even just two moon cycles ago? She'd learned all those things, taking to them with remarkable speed.

Perhaps she could adapt to become a passable parent.

Sorac deserved that much from her. If it didn't turn out, she'd worry about that later.

Hoisting herself up the rim of the nest, she swung a leg over and landed in the sand. Once she straightened and dusted the sand from her pants, she moved toward the nearest egg and gently rested a hand against it to feel the life within.

Now, what would the firedrake do? He'd likely already turned them before he'd left to get sand. He sometimes sang to them, she remembered.

Singing wouldn't do any harm.

A gentle smile touched her lips, and after a moment she sang. Her tune was a lament, a song about mourning the loss of friends and allies after some ancient battle. It was haunting, and she hoped the chicks sleeping inside their eggs thought the same.

It was probably more suitable than a jaunty drinking song. The only other kind she knew.

She was singing the refrain a fourth time when Sorac returned, his great wing membranes cupped to hold sand like two giant shovels. Once he reached her side, he halted, just listening, his task forgotten.

She could see it in his wide unfocused eyes.

When she finished, he gave himself a little shake.

"Are you sure you're not half siren?" he asked as he deposited the first load of sand.

"There was one a few generations back on my mother's side."

He snorted. "I was just joking, but that explains why I've always loved to hear you sing. You don't do it enough."

"I suppose I shall have to sing more if it pleases you and the unhatched drakelings. Otherwise, I'll be forced to witness that hideous sulking face of yours."

"Thank you... I think." He returned to working on his nest only to pause and glance up at her, his expression full of eagerness. "It occurs to me that I haven't made myself as available as I should. Do you need to feed?"

She pushed aside her first response, which was to laugh at his eagerness. But it was a valid question, and the truth was she would need to feed sometime in the next day or two. She'd been making do by draining the sexual energy the humans gave off. It sustained her but wasn't filling.

"I wouldn't mind borrowing you for an hour or two later tonight."

"Only an hour," he laughed. "That's hardly worth the effort. Why don't I make myself available from sunset until dawn?"

Vaspara grinned. "That appeals to me."

"Good. I will—" Sorac was cut short by a ghostly sound.

She took three steps back and had her sword out before she realized where the sound originated.

One of the eggs vibrated gently as the tiny firedrake inside sang the last few notes of Vaspara's song back to her. The eerily beautiful sound did something strange to her heart, and for no reason she could discern, tears sprung to her eyes.

Tears. Of all the foolish, knobheaded....

"Mattis says his son needs help with framing. I should go." She turned and had fled ten paces when she forced herself to stop and call over her shoulder. "I'll see you later tonight."

"I'll be ready." Sorac's simple words were full of thoughtful overtones.

He knew her too well and must sense something had her off balance. She knew it, too. She just didn't know how to regain her equilibrium.

CHAPTER TWELVE

Sorac washed up after a long afternoon of splitting planks to use as rafters in the village. He glanced at the horizon through the trees and noted the lateness of the hour. The sun was almost touching the ocean.

Time had slipped away from him, but he certainly hadn't forgotten Vaspara had said she'd be coming to him tonight. That had filled his thoughts as he'd labored throughout the day. He'd had to work in his human form, realizing too late he hadn't thought to make firedrake-sized tools for the task, and Mattis, Kierdan, and Callum needed the rafters for tomorrow.

But the cool stream had revived him well enough. Soon Vaspara would be here, and he'd be fully rejuvenated by the time she left him at dawn.

Thinking of all the ways he and Vaspara could spend the night, Sorac walked back up the slope toward his nest while half in a dream. He'd almost reached his destination when a loud whistle rang through the air. He grinned and turned to where Vaspara was leaning against a tree along the side of the path.

He'd been so distracted by thoughts of her, he hadn't even realized the object of his imagination had arrived.

"How long have you been there?" he asked, pretending boredom.

"Long enough to see you strip and walk into the stream." Vaspara grinned, her gaze traveling up and down his body.

"I was just heading back to the nest for a clean pair of pants and a bite to eat."

"Mmm. Don't get dressed on my account." Vaspara fell in beside him as he climbed the sloping trail.

Grinning, he glanced sidelong at her but had to wait a few moments for her gaze to travel back up before he could catch her eye. He recognized her look of hunger.

Pleasure that it was for him washed through his mind and body.

"I'm not going to make it back to the nest, am I?" he stated with a wink.

"Smart lizard," Vaspara purred.

Between one step and the next, she pounced, her hands reaching for his shoulders, fingers digging into his scales and gripping the short spikes. She used her considerable strength to shove him up against a tree. A moment later her lips were crushed against his in a heated kiss while she tore the clothing from her body.

He enjoyed Vaspara's fire and dominance. It was a part

of her personality. But had he wanted, he could have put up a fight, the two of them wrestling for control—a contest where he wasn't sure which of them would win—but that's not what he wanted this time.

Later, once they'd both taken the edge off, there could be gentleness. Or maybe a wrestling match, he mused with a grin. But Vaspara soon drove thoughts of anything but this moment out of his mind.

She was fierce and wanton this time, touching him everywhere, pressing her curves against him, using her considerable strength and skill to demand he give her everything. When he was too slow, she climbed him and impaled herself on his aching length.

He groaned and arched up into her, his head falling back to smash against the tree trunk behind him. The slight pain only made what he was feeling that much clearer. Vaspara must have felt his rising desperation for she wordlessly demanded his surrender.

With a growl, he gave her what she asked for, as hard and fast as he could.

"Sorac," she purred his name, her emotions suddenly flooding into him. "So perfect."

As the wave of her love and desire swamped him, he snarled and pushed off from the tree, carrying her to the forest floor where he pinned her to the ground.

Something else rose up within him, a power born of his fiery elemental magic. This was a firedrake's need. The strength of it surprised him, nearly obliterating higher thought, but he retained enough wherewithal to know what this was.

Firedrake mating instincts.

This had just crossed from sex and feeding into something much more life-altering.

"Vaspara, do you want me?" he asked as he hunched over her, driving deep.

"Goddess, yes."

His lust-fogged mind realized she might not understand what he was asking. "Do you want this? Do you want me forever?"

"Forever might just be long enough for me to get my fill of you." Her fangs flashed and then she was biting down on the vulnerable spot just above his shoulder spikes where the scales were thinner.

He jerked, his entire body tensing and trembling, but he managed to hold back his release as Vaspara found her peak.

She didn't understand what he was asking. He needed to make her understand.

A moment later she purred and licked at the few drops of blood beading up on his skin, the compound in her saliva already working to heal the small wound. "You taste divine. Must be your father's blood."

She started moving against him again.

He needed to tell her, but he realized he feared her response. It was why he hadn't pressed the issue during the other feedings, but now his firedrake nature was making him face this head on.

Divine Ones give me strength and please be merciful.

He was out of time and just blurted the words. "My mate. Do you want to be my mate? Mother to my drakelings?"

"What?" Her startled response sank in slowly. If that hadn't been enough for him to understand, her horrified look would have done the job.

"My firedrake nature wants more than sex. I want you to be my mate, mother to my drakelings. Please, I know it isn't fair to ask you this now, but I can't pretend anymore."

"No," Vaspara said weakly. She'd stopped moving, stopped touching him with passion. The lack left him both aching and cold. The look in her eyes was now a mix of terror and horror. It matched the earlier tone in her voice. "No! I don't want to be a mother. Never."

She pushed at his shoulder, shoving him back, scrambling out from under him.

"Tell me you didn't just impregnate me!" She backed away from him.

He shook his head. "No, you're safe from that."

"Good." She leaned down and swiftly gathered her clothing. "I don't want that, Sorac. I'll never want that. I'm sorry if you didn't understand that. I wasn't trying to lead you on. Perhaps I should have made myself clearer in some way, so there was no doubt in your mind. I'm sorry."

She turned and walked away, and he was sure she'd just taken some vital part of him with her.

Drawing his legs up under him, he just sat for a few moments, wondering how everything had gone so horribly wrong so quickly.

"Why didn't I just keep my mouth shut?"

But he already knew the answer. He couldn't lie to Vaspara, couldn't take her as his mate without giving her a choice. If he had, in fifty years, when his fertility cycle was upon him again, his firedrake nature would overrule his control and seek out his mate to start their next clutch. And Vaspara wouldn't be able to resist his power.

His fertility god heritage would seduce her into compliance.

He would never willingly harm Vaspara. Now all he could do was watch as she fled him, taking a piece of his heart with her.

Sorac glanced down at his hands and started to grieve for what he'd lost and what he'd now never have because he'd failed to win the heart of a succubus.

Was such a thing even possible?

CHAPTER THIRTEEN

She'd never run from an opponent in her life, Vaspara mused sourly. Yet, she now fled, if not an adversary, then something far more dangerous to her wellbeing and peace of mind.

Bloody plagues and blight! He'd asked her to be his mate, to be the mother to his drakelings, and she'd turned into a coward at the mere thought.

"They'll just hatch into little ones. Not some monstrous soul-sucking monstrosity. Why can't I just stand and face this challenge with dignity?"

It wasn't like she hadn't trained thousands of youths, turning them into warriors. The drakelings couldn't be that different, could they?

"Goddess, I'll break them, or ruin them, or fail both them or Sorac in some other fashion."

"What is this?" asked a male voice rich with humor. "Is this the normally silent and stoic Vaspara I see talking to herself as she flees through the forest? Fleeing from a certain Firedrake and his brood?"

Vaspara skidded to a halt and sought the direction of the voice. It echoed from all directions at once. She'd spent enough time with the djinn to have grown familiar with his habit of speaking before taking solid form.

She waited for him to show himself.

Her patience was rewarded a moment later. Bright light with a molten metal quality shifted and shimmered in the air a few body-lengths in front of her. Magic continued to spin outward from a dense point in the center, increasing in quantity. Soon the vague shape took on the djinn's familiar and cruelly handsome features.

She and the other island residents had grown somewhat accustomed to the djinn, and Vaspara fisted her hand against her hips. "You were watching Sorac and me?"

The thought of him watching their mating didn't bother Vaspara. It was the conversation afterward, and her shame, she would have kept private.

The djinn shuddered. "Listening actually. Most unwillingly. But since Sorac insists on keeping my bottle near his nest, I didn't have a choice. A djinn hears all that goes on outside his bottle."

"Well, you can just go and pretend like you didn't hear anything."

"It might go against common beliefs about my kind but simply wishing to unhear something doesn't make it happen, not even for a djinn."

Grunting, Vaspara continued down the path on her way to the beach, fervently hoping the djinn wouldn't follow.

Of course he did. She tried to ignore him.

When she reached the beach, she wasn't the only person with that idea. Mattis was sitting next to a bonfire, watching the ocean waves crashing into shore. Feeling less social than usual, Vaspara was tempted to turn and vanish back into the tree line, but Mattis glanced up and waved her over before she could make her escape.

Besides, she already had the djinn trailing along beside her. Perhaps she could scrape him off on the human. The djinn often spent time with the elder, the two of them telling each other stories.

With a new motive, Vaspara joined Mattis, intent on getting the human and the djinn talking. Later, Vaspara would sneak away while they were distracted.

She glanced over her shoulder at the djinn to behold a delighted glint in his eyes. Instantly, her expression turned sour, her lips compressing into a thin line of unhappiness.

"Mattis, I think we need to sit Captain Vaspara down and have a talk with her. She's on a path to create an enormous rift between herself and Sorac."

Mattis looked up at the djinn. "You don't say?"

Next, the elder leaned back and studied Vaspara without a hint of surprise. Somehow the human knew of her problems. How? Vaspara had been very careful to keep her relationship with Sorac the same as always. Well, except for the feedings.

Vaspara tried to ignore Mattis's attempts at catching her eye.

With a huff, the human pointed a finger at her and then one of the three smooth, bark-stripped tree trunks they used as temporary benches around the fire. "Sit and talk. The night's not getting any younger. Neither am I."

"It's not your concern."

Nor is it yours either, Vaspara thought as she aimed a glower at the meddling djinn.

"Of course it is. I've known you all my life, and I think I speak for us both when I say we are old friends. Friends help each other. Speak. Perhaps there is something I can help you with."

Deciding it was better to get it over with, she sat.

The djinn settled on a log on the opposite side of the fire. "Perhaps there is some bit of wisdom I can share as well. Speak succubus."

"Why do you care?" Vaspara bit out, her comment directed at the djinn. "You aren't even mortal."

"No, but love transcends all three realms. Being of the Spirit Realm doesn't exclude me from that condition, and even I know love isn't finite."

"What's he droning on about?" Mattis asked.

"I don't have a clue," Vaspara lied.

The djinn's grin only grew broader. "The captain is afraid of motherhood for two reasons. First, she doubts if she has enough love for all of them. Which is foolish. Haven't I already stated that love isn't finite?"

Mattis just shook his head at the djinn.

For his part, the djinn ignored the human and continued his explanation. "Second, she thinks she'll somehow damage the young drakelings emotionally if she agrees to become their mother as Sorac hopes." The djinn laughed. "Raising children can't be that difficult compared to life within the Battle Goddess's kingdom, surely?"

"Have you ever raised even one child?" she snapped back.

He looked startled for a moment before the light of amusement reentered his eyes. "I have not yet had that ordeal thrust upon me."

"Hah. Your words speak volumes. You know even less about children than I do. Go sit this conversation out." She made shooing gestures, but he didn't take the hint.

The djinn's amusement grew. "Perhaps I shall help you and the firedrake raise these little ones."

"Three more unprepared parents the universe shall never see," Mattis muttered.

"See, Djinn! Even the human thinks I'll be a disaster."

Mattis just rolled his eyes. "That's not what I said. You can learn. Just like you've learned other things since coming here, you'll learn from your mistakes. Children are resilient."

The djinn laughed, mirth making his tattoos flare hotter and brighter. "We'll either raise stunningly brilliant offspring, well versed in the universe's lore—"

Vaspara cut him off. "Or we'll raise the greatest tyrants the universe has ever known."

The djinn shrugged. "There is always that possibility if you wish that to be their path."

Her lips compressed. Was he joking? She couldn't tell.

"Gods," Mattis snorted and chuckled. "If you want them to be good, merely lavish them with love and teach them right from wrong to the best of your abilities."

"All of what you said—that's the part I think I'll fail at." Vaspara braced her hands on either side of her hips and dug her claws into the smooth surface of the stout trunk that served as her seat.

"Listen here," Mattis said, his voice changing to the one he often used on misbehaving younglings. "I've raised enough children, grandchildren, and soon great-grandchildren to be a bit of an expert on the subject. I will ask you some questions, and you will give me honest answers. Afterward, I'll tell you if you'll be a good parent or not. Do you agree to my terms?"

"I... Fine. Ask your questions."

"Good." Mattis poured himself some tea. He took a swallow, rolled his eyes, and muttered about what dastardly fate had brought him to this point of counseling a succubus. "Do you love Sorac?"

Frowning at the fire, she only now realized how hard this would be. After a long sigh, she answered the human's question. "You know I do."

"Do you wish to spend your life with Sorac?"

"Yes."

"And I know you're aware it won't just be Sorac you will spend your life with."

"Of course. That's what I'm terrified of mucking up. That's why I'm here."

Mattis took another gulp of tea. "I'm aware. Just making sure you truly know what's at stake. Now you have a decision to make. One only you can make. Sorac will be a father. The drakelings are a part of his future. You must decide how much you want to be a part of Sorac's life. Do you want to be his friend? Or his mate?"

"I don't know. That's why I ran tonight."

"You'll find it very difficult to run from the drakelings once they hatch. We live on an island." Mattis laughed and then turned reflective. "Perhaps you can still keep something of the deep bond you share with Sorac with no need to also be the drakelings' mother, or perhaps you can't. What is between you and Sorac may not survive if you can't love something that is so much a part of him."

That hadn't even occurred to Vaspara. It should have. They were now deep in firedrake territory. If she shunned him, he might go seek out one of his own kind.

"You need to decide if your fear of motherhood is greater than your fear of losing Sorac's love. Can you live without that deep bond? And last, can you accept that he'll love them as much or more than you?" Mattis paused and looked at his cup, mumbling about needing something stronger than tea. With a grunt, he looked back up. "If you can't share him, then you would be better to break things off with him now. Don't make him be the one to choose between the woman he loves and his little ones. That would be cruel, and as harsh as your life has made you, you were never cruel."

A chill raced down her spine at the thought of losing what she and Sorac shared. Oh, she'd known they would likely die in battle one day, but when it happened, she planned for them to be fighting shoulder to shoulder. They'd face what came next together like they always had.

But what if their deep bond faded and their bodies

lived on, existing day to day? A hollow pit opened in her soul at the thought. She couldn't face a long existence without her firedrake partner.

That new fear swiftly eclipsed every other doubt she'd had in the last few days. She was on her feet and striding away from the beach before she'd fully formed a coherent thought.

Mattis raised his voice and called out after her, "If you love Sorac enough to love his drakelings as well, then you will make a fine mother."

The nesting area was just coming into view when the haunting song of the drakelings singing started up. Her heart did that strange little flip at hearing the melody again. As she hurried toward the nest, she realized they weren't singing to her this time.

Sorac, having returned to his firedrake form, had curled his body around the eggs, his head pressed against them, eyes closed. Everything about his hunched position spoke of his pain. A firedrake might not cry, but he was suffering.

Vaspara continued to stride forward. Once she reached him, she pressed herself against his warm scales and wrapped her arms around as much of his tapered muzzle as she could reach.

"I'm sorry that I've been an idiot. I love you, and I'll love your drakelings, too." She fought back a wave of foolish tears and muttered, "I'm already starting to love them, and I haven't even met them yet. That scared me, and I ran. I'm sorry I was such a knobheaded coward."

She was mumbling now but didn't care.

Sorac rumbled happily as one of his massive hands

closed around her to hold her in place while he nuzzled her gently, bathing her in his warm, steamy breath.

"Don't cook me, you great lizard. It will be a little difficult to be the mother to your drakelings if I'm a ghost."

The firedrake made a soft, emotional snort and more steam and a few flames licked around his teeth.

"Seriously, don't cook me, Lizardman."

"My fire won't hurt you. My magic already considers you my mate; you're immune to its destructive power."

"Glad to hear I won't accidentally get cooked, but even if I weren't immune, it wouldn't change my mind. I'd still love you and the little ones, too." She reached out and trailed her fingers down the pebbly shell of the nearest egg, the beat of the drakelings heart a soft pulse against her fingertips. Soon the one inside sang again, and more foolish tears flowed down her cheeks.

"I don't know what kind of witchery you and these drakelings have woven over me, but I'll be your mate and grow into the mother they need."

"No witchery," Sorac rumbled, the tone deep and soothing. "Just love."

"I'll do my best by them and you," Vaspara said with a self-deprecating snort. "But don't expect perfection. I'm not mother material. There will be lots of blunders and learning."

"For me as well. We'll blunder together." Flames burst from between his scales and licked along them for a moment, and then the firedrake shifted back into the form of a man.

He grinned, looking both eager and uncertain. "If I

recall, we were in the middle of something before I frightened you off earlier with all my demands. I hate leaving things unfinished."

Vaspara stepped into Sorac's embrace and was delighted he hadn't bothered to summon clothing or armor. It would have slowed her down too much, and at this moment, she needed to feel the brush of his skin against hers more than she needed to breathe.

Their kisses and caresses soon turned heated, and Sorac was stripping her out of her clothing with quick, sure motions. She was usually the aggressor in sex, and would be again later, but right this moment, she sensed Sorac's fire-drake nature was clamoring to claim her as his mate.

He carried them to the ground, his weight settling over her. When he aligned them, she wrapped her legs around his hips and growled out encouragement, letting him know she was pleased with the pace he'd set.

There would be time for gentleness later. Grinning, she bit down on his shoulder, her teeth pinching and scraping but not piercing the skin, not yet.

Sorac rumbled out something very lizardish at the press of her teeth.

Holding him in a fierce embrace, she enjoyed having the big male's body working in unison with hers, lust and magic flowing between them.

"You are addictive," she whispered.

Sorac lifted his lips away from her skin long enough to mumble, "Good. I want to provide you with something else no other male ever has or ever will."

Stroking a hand down his spine, she smiled against his

throat. "You already do that every day. You're my partner, guardian of my heart." She paused and glanced sideways at the nearest egg. "The father of our future children."

The firedrake rumbled something heated against her skin, and after that, there was no more talking.

Much later, Vaspara lay curled against Sorac's side. He slept heavily in the way of a fully sated male. Rare moments like this only made her value the precious time they had together. If the gods were kind, there would be many more moments like this one.

She smiled up at the bright stars slowly spinning across the heavens as she lay awake listening to Sorac's deep, even breathing. She brushed her mind against his shields and his mental barriers dropped, allowing their minds to mingle.

Vaspara basked in the evidence of his absolute trust in her. Her smile grew broader when she realized he was dreaming about her and his drakelings. In the dream, his entire family was on the smooth sands of the southern side of the island where the beaches were wide and mostly free of rocks.

She, Sorac, and his drakelings were racing and playing in the surf. The innocence of the scene wasn't something she'd ever thought possible in her life, but perhaps it was. All she had to do was reach out and take it.

Vaspara smiled once more at Sorac's dream and then turned to look at the eggs. One was within touching distance, and she stroked her fingertips along the warm shell.

"I may be a disaster as a mother, but I'm a fierce bitch and know how to destroy my enemies. I give you my promise, as long as I draw breath, I will keep you and all your brothers and sisters safe. You will know love and safety. Rest, grow strong, and when you are ready, I'll be here waiting."

CHAPTER FOURTEEN

After one final glower at the vines, Vaspara shoved the tangled mass off her lap and leaned back against the log bench.

Who would have thought weaving and knotting vines together to make a fish trap would be so complicated? But in the four moon cycles they'd been living on the island, she'd never mastered the art of weaving things together.

"I'd fight for the chance to kill something," she muttered to herself.

Rising, she moved toward a small cooking fire she'd started earlier and poured herself a cup of tea. Taking a sip, she wished for mulled wine. Or something stronger, but the only thing they had on the island was water and a dwindling supply of dried herbs.

At least they had their freedom, she thought as she glowered down at the weak tea in her cup. Perhaps in a few months they could venture forth, exploring the surrounding islands and the land mass far to the west. There were other kingdoms near. And where civilization existed, there was usually some form of fermented drink to be had.

She'd discuss the possibility of looking into trade later, once Sorac was finished putting a roof on the most recent structure under construction. The firedrake was much stronger than the rest of them, and when he was in his true form, he was better than scaffolding or ramps.

A sudden, sharp crack caught her attention. She looked toward the nest. The sound came again. A moment later, she bolted to her feet in understanding. Rushing to the nest, she hauled herself over the stout wall and dropped down into the hot sand.

Scanning each of the eggs, searching for the source of the noise, she circled the nest. The sound came a third time, and she spotted one egg with a small, but widening, crack running outward from a tiny hole near the top. A little curl of fire licked up from the hole as the baby fire-drake inside expressed his annoyance at not yet having broken free.

"Sorac," she called, using magic to touch his mind. "You great lizard. Get your big, scaly backside to the nest now! One of the eggs is hatching! I don't know what to do!"

She didn't care if she sounded panicked.

"I'm on my way." His excitement speared into her mind, a living fire that forked and snapped like lightning through her senses.

It didn't hurt. He hadn't lied when he said his power could no longer harm her now that they were mates. In the days following their mating, she'd learned firedrakes forged powerful mating bonds that allowed either member of the pair to call upon the other's power in times of need or in defense of the nest.

As he'd promised, the big firedrake was soon winging toward her location, his shadow racing ahead of him across the island. With a great flapping of wings and swirling sand, he came in for a landing at the edge of the nest.

After only the barest acknowledgment of her presence, he nosed at the eggs until he found the one with the crack. Snorting softly, he flicked his tongue out, scenting his child. Then Sorac crooned softly to his hatching, singing encouragements.

The egg rocked and shook with the hatchling's vigorous pecking. Soon a small pointed muzzle poked from the egg. A moment later, the drakeling shifted to press an eyeball against the opening. It looked directly at her.

"Hello, little one," she called softly. "Welcome to the world."

Inside the egg, the hatchling made an excited cry loud enough to make her ears throb.

"My son has good lungs." Sorac rumbled with laughter.

"The little one is male?"

"Yes," Sorac nodded, dipping his muzzle close to the egg for another sniff. "His scent is male. My first born is a son." Pride colored his tone.

"Our son," Vaspara corrected gently.

Sorac's large pupils expanded at her words, turning his eyes entirely black for a moment. Stretching his long neck, he brought his muzzle in close and rubbed it against her chest.

"Our son," he agreed, sounding happier than she'd ever recalled.

As the hatchling continued to fight his way out of his shell, Vaspara glanced at the other eggs. "How long before they hatch?"

"It'll be three days before the next is ready to hatch." Sorac nudged the egg to the immediate right of the one hatching. "After I acquired each egg from the mother, I put it in the nest and took down the stasis spell so they could absorb my magic for three days before restoring the spell, halting their development. A new hatchling will emerge from his or her egg every three days."

The egg in the nest's center rolled suddenly, and with a mighty screech, two tiny wings burst out from inside, shattering the shell. Suddenly finding itself free, the baby drake stretched full length in the sand.

Sorac crooned and nuzzled the little one and then tilted his head to look at Vaspara.

Moment of truth, Vaspara thought as a nervous thrill slid through her middle. Coming to the little drake's side, she knelt and held a hand out for him to sniff. He loosed the same cry he'd made when he'd first looked at her through the small hole in his egg.

"That cry means mother," Sorac explained.

Vaspara felt her jaw drop. "They already recognize me?"

"They imprinted upon your magic and essence while still in the egg."

Reaching out, she stroked a finger down the little

drakeling's head. His scales were still a muddy sort of olive shade, but according to his shell color and pattern, he'd turn a bright jewel blue with a hint of black at the tips of his scales when he was older.

His wings seemed small compared to his body. She touched each one gently, fearing there was something wrong.

Sorac nuzzled the drakeling. "His wings will soon expand now that he is free of his shell."

Vaspara nodded as she continued her exploration of the tiny but perfect hatchling. His tail was twice the length of his body and his four little legs with their clawed tips were already strong and able to carry him short distances.

He called to her again and then wriggled closer. Soon he was in her lap, pressing his head against her middle. Her arms closed around him and her heart did that strange flutter as tears gathered in her eyes.

"I've got you," she whispered softly. She had indeed fallen far in such a short time, but she couldn't find it in her to wish back the old Vaspara.

"He'll be hungry in a matter of moments. I'll grab a fish from the stock pond." Sorac abandoned her with the little drakeling.

They'd been saving some of their catch and putting them in a special salt-water pond they'd created so they could have fresh food nearby when the drakelings hatched. Sorac had explained, the drakeling would be ravenous within moments of hatching. They'd decided it was best to have fresh food at hand, since the hatchlings wouldn't eat cooked or dried meat.

The drakeling rested his head between her breasts, one ear pressed to her heart, his big, jet-black eyes watching her. He was such a darling she grinned like a fool. "Your father will bring something back shortly."

As promised, Sorac soon returned with a fish. He dropped it next to Vaspara and then looked at her expectantly.

Reluctantly, she placed the hatchling on the sand close to the fish and waited for Sorac to tear the fish into bite-sized pieces.

"Female firedrakes are protective of their hatchlings and rarely allow their mates to feed the young for the first few days." Sorac grinned at her look of surprise. "He's waiting for you to shred the fish."

She glanced down at the fish. Well, she had said she wanted to kill something, hadn't she? A hapless fish hadn't been quite what she had in mind.

With a shrug, she swiftly dealt the fish a death blow and then unsheathed her claws. Butchering the fish was swift work, and soon she was feeding tidbits of meat to the excited hatchling. He was as hungry as Sorac said he would be.

Once he'd eaten the entire fish, he waddled over to Vaspara and climbed into her lap, where he soon fell asleep.

"You did that well," Sorac said, his voice a heated rumble near her ear. He was lying down with his body curled around her and the eggs, his head situated so he could peer over her shoulder and gaze at his son.

She rolled her eyes. "It was one fish. Not a battle against our greatest foes."

Sorac chuckled. "Still, I think motherhood will suit you."

He was partly correct. Motherhood might still scare her, she admitted, but she would master this raising of drakelings like everything else she'd put her mind to. She didn't believe in failure. Only practice and eventual success.

She'd succeed at this as well.

CHAPTER FIFTEEN

After a little over a month's time, all fourteen of his eggs had hatched. Each drakeling was as healthy and perfectly formed as the first. Sorac was pleased beyond measure with his brood. And Vaspara, too.

She'd adapted to motherhood and this new island life better than he'd thought.

Oh, like him, she was ever vigilant. Instincts usually had her hand settling on her sword's hilt every time a problem arose, but she'd always come around, and together they always found a solution to whatever problem had occurred.

As much as he loved his new life, day to day living on the island was exhausting and challenging.

The drakelings added to the chaos. They liked to escape their nest and chase after the djinn when he was off helping the humans. Sorac thought his drakelings might view the djinn as walking, talking food. For his part, the djinn didn't seem to mind that they chased him around and siphoned magical energy from him as often as he allowed.

Other times, Sorac or Vaspara would wake from a nap or some other distraction to find the hatchlings had escaped their nest and were exploring their surroundings on their own. It was good firedrakes were immune to snake venom, even young drakes were impervious.

As for the big cats, the only other large predator on the island, they steered clear of Sorac's domain. So, while hunting down his escaped drakelings could be an exercise in frustration, they weren't really in danger.

He had no complaints with his life.

Today, he was in his natural form again, working near the island's eastern beach, felling trees they'd later use for building fishing boats and a dock. Vaspara was laboring alongside Callum, Kierdan, and Sylas stripping bark and limbs from the trees Sorac had pulled from the ground.

Alaya and her two children, Tristan and Myrandis, were working on bundling together long grass that they'd later use for thatching roofs.

While back at the nest, the djinn and Mattis were watching over and entertaining the drakelings.

Vaspara set aside the long blade she was using to strip bark and approached his position. "If you've flexed your muscles enough for one morning, we'd like to break for a midday meal. Besides, I should check to see if Mattis needs anything."

He was just nodding agreement when the defensive spells he and Vaspara had woven around the islands all flared at once.

Spinning in a half-circle and displacing a cloud of sand, he faced the direction of the nest, the same direction the disturbance originated.

"That's a portal spell," Vaspara shouted as she ran up the slope.

Sorac flared his wings wide. "Stay here," he shouted at the humans. "The spell is cutting through the defenses like they're vapor. It has to be blood magic."

Breaking into a gallop, he darted down the beach and launched himself into the air, his wings pounding as if he flew headlong into storm winds. Terror drove him forward. Terror for his little ones and what the blood witch would do to them.

Somewhere below Vaspara was shouting his name, but he didn't have time to double back and snatch her. He had to reach his drakelings.

The treeless hilltop where he'd built his nest soon came into sight. Roaring, he dropped out of the sky and landed heavily on the hillside, but captains Taryin and Bervicta had already prepared for his attack with a company of the Battle Goddess's best warriors circling his nest.

Seeing his little ones captured and wrapped in spells of restraint triggered a deep rage that overrode his fear. He snarled and advanced, elemental fire waking deep within.

"I would not, Sorac, not if you care for your young." Taryin craned her neck to look up at him. As she did, she gently ran a hand over the head of one of the drakelings, his firstborn, Sandorian.

She could kill the little one with a moment's thought.

Still growling, he backed up three steps. "Don't hurt them."

"That's better. Was that so hard?"

Yes, he thought. *Not attacking and tearing you limb from limb is very, very hard.*

He forced his mind to calm as he took in the scene in more detail. The blood witch had the djinn's bottle tucked into her top. He almost hadn't noticed, but now that he saw it, his eyes sought the djinn.

Sorac found him farther back, behind Taryin, her skirts partly obscuring his hunched form. He'd curled forward on the ground, almost like he was bowing, but the power rippling along his form told a different story. The djinn was fighting his own magic, battling the spell of enslavement.

It was equally clear he was losing that battle. The strain was tearing his corporeal form to shreds.

"I've never read about a djinn fighting a compulsion so hard." Taryin half turned. "He can't win, and yet he tries to break free to aid these young creatures."

The witch's expression said the djinn's wish to aid them confounded her.

But Sorac understood. It might go against everything they thought they knew about a djinn, but this one loved the little drakelings in his own way.

After a moment, the blood witch looked down at the drakeling she held in her arms and then back at the djinn. "Ah. I think I understand now, though, I'm not sure I believe it."

She turned and threaded her way through the soldiers,

only pausing to call back to Sorac. "You, stay where you are and don't move if you want all your young to survive."

Continuing toward the djinn, she circled the spirit creature a few times. "You will obey me. You must. You have no other choice."

"There is always a choice," the djinn barked back.

The blood witch just grinned and shook her head. "Not for you. Not if you don't want to watch me kill this sweet little fellow right in front of you."

She gestured one soldier closer and whispered in his ear. He nodded and drew his dagger.

Sorac howled as the male pressed his blade against the drakeling's throat. The little one hissed, sensing danger, but he couldn't move.

Roaring, Sorac advanced.

"I told you not to move," the blood witch barked. All the guards holding drakelings drew their daggers. "You can't save them all. If you attack, you might save none. Same goes for you, djinn. Stop fighting, or I'll kill this one and his blood will be on your hands."

The djinn didn't answer in words, but as he slowly forced himself off the ground, Sorac could see the look of defeat in the male's fiery gaze. Some battles had to be lost to win the war. Sorac knew that, but it didn't make this surrender any easier.

"As my mistress commands," the djinn said, his voice cold enough to slay.

Blood Witch Taryin turned to Sorac next, her one eyebrow raised in question. "And you? Are you prepared to surrender, drake?"

Biting off another snarl building in his chest, Sorac answered. "I'll do what you want. Just don't harm my drakelings."

"Shift back into your man form," Taryin ordered.

Swallowing back his fire, he battled instincts and forced his firedrake nature to give over and resumed the form of a man. "I'll return with you peacefully; just don't kill them."

"Good. You were always wise, Sorac. But I don't want your surrender. I need something else. Remember, if you fight or resist, I'll kill this little one."

The blood witch turned her attention back to the djinn. "You, kill the firedrake."

earing Taryin's command, Vaspara hurtled herself over the berm she'd been hiding behind. She would not lose Sorac or her family. Summoning the full force of her magic, everything she possessed, she dragged it out from the deepest recesses of her soul.

Flinging it toward Sorac with all her love and desperation, she issued only one command: protect.

A shield of shimmering radiance surrounded the firedrake a moment before the djinn's spell struck. The two powers exploded outward in a fiery brilliance, blinding Vaspara.

But she didn't need her sight to beg.

"Don't kill him. He's worth more to you alive than dead. He can train the little ones as they grow. The Battle Goddess can have the winged legion she's always wanted."

The other soldiers were in chaos. Vaspara could hear their shouts, curses, and grunts as they stumbled blindly.

But then something else distracted her as the hair on her arms stood erect.

The djinn was calling more magic. He wasn't blinded like the rest of them she realized in despair. She didn't have it in her to summon a second defensive shield.

Sorac would die this time.

"I love you and the drakelings," she whispered into his mind.

"You made my existence worth living, my beloved succubus, my oldest friend. I'll see you in the afterlife one day."

"We'll go together," she said as she stumbled toward him.

"No, Vaspara. If they let you live, try to find a way to still be the mother to my brood." Then his tail knocked her off her feet, preventing her from reaching him. *"Goodbye, my love."*

No! Everything within her cried out.

"Hold!" The blood witch's sharp command held Vaspara frozen even though the command was for the djinn, not her.

Slowly Vaspara's sight returned, grainy and colorless.

Taryin was approaching her.

"How did you stop a djinn's spell? The first blow should have cut right through your magic and killed the firedrake."

"I don't know." That was the truth. She wasn't sure where the power had come from.

"She loves the firedrake more than she loves her own soul," said the djinn in his coldly cruel voice. "That gave her the ability to tap into the essence of her soul—spirit magic, similar to what I command."

The blood witch tilted her head, studying them both. "I wish to know more about this ability."

"Why?" the djinn asked. "Love is not something you will ever be able to mimic or even understand."

"If there is a power that can stand against a djinn's magic, then I must know more about such an ability. The succubus and the firedrake can both live for now."

Vaspara continued to blink. Slowly color returned to her vision.

Taryin was now watching her with a calculating eye. "Together we will dig until we find the answers I seek."

"Might I offer a suggestion, mistress." The djinn made the title sound like an insult, but he didn't seem to care what the blood witch might do in retaliation. "Has not the Battle Goddess always wanted a flying legion? I've studied Sorac enough to know he wouldn't do anything to endanger his drakelings. He'll obey whatever orders you issue without question."

"Hmm. I see a flaw with your reasoning, djinn," Taryin challenged. "If he is flying with his legion of firedrakes, whatever can we use to hold him? He and his children can just fly off at any moment."

"You use me," Vaspara said suddenly, her voice growing stronger as she walked toward the blood witch's location. "He's been in love with me for a thousand years, hoping, yearning, dreaming of the day I'd accept him as my mate and help him raise his brood. I agreed. We formed mating bonds. Now he will do whatever he must to protect me."

Vaspara had promised the drakelings she'd be a fiercely protective mother. Now it was time to prove it by surrendering her freedom to save their father "Take me back to the fortress. Lock me in a dark cell. You'll be able to use me against Sorac. To protect me and the little ones, he'll do anything you want. Killing him would be a great waste."

Taryin looked thoughtful, so Vaspara continued. "He'll train his drakelings in the ways of war. It will be what the Lady of Battles always wanted. He'll raise as many broods as she allows."

"It's true," Sorac said, joining the conversation. "Keep Vaspara as a slave. Just don't kill her. I'll do as the Battle Goddess wishes, breed who and however many females she demands. I'll raise legion after legion of firedrakes for her to use in her wars. All of them will serve the goddess."

The blood witch snorted and turned her gaze back to Vaspara "Very well, we will do as you and your firedrake lover suggest. Though after a few centuries trapped in the darkness below the dungeons, you might look back at this day and wish I'd killed you both instead."

Vaspara knew she'd never regret saving Sorac and their family. It didn't matter what they did to her, that would never change.

"Harpy, come and collar these two traitors."

Looking unhappier than Vaspara had ever seen, Bervicta approached Sorac and snapped a collar in place around his neck. Distractedly Vaspara noted it was like the ones Gryton had created to use on the Avatars.

Once Sorac was trapped, Bervicta approached Vaspara next, swiftly securing a collar to her neck.

She smelled and tasted the blood witch's taint as they bound Vaspara's magic far beyond her reach.

Leaning forward, the harpy brought her lips close to Vaspara's ear. "I'm sorry. I'll do all I can to make sure the little ones are well cared for."

Vaspara didn't let her expression betray even a hint of the relief she felt at her friend's words. Harpies were heartless and vicious in many ways, but they were devoted to their young. If Bervicta said she'd do her best to look after the little ones, she would. She'd likely adopt them herself if the Battle Goddess allowed.

"Come. I have been away long enough these past months hunting for you," Taryin called as she turned her back on them and attended to the waiting portal spell that still glowed with power. "Bring the prisoners and let us return home. I've learned much I must tell the Battle Goddess."

The soldiers formed up. The ones holding the drakelings kept themselves away from Sorac and Vaspara. As Bervicta marched her toward the open portal spell, the djinn caught Vaspara's attention with a slight bow in her direction.

She met his gaze.

"Succubus, I lacked the opportunity to escape with the drakelings," the djinn whispered into her mind. *"For that, I'll be eternally sorry, but if it's any compensation, I managed to shield Mattis and the others. It was the least I could do for their friendship and kindness."*

"Thank you."

Guilt bled off the djinn. *"The portal opened almost on top of the nest. It's my fault you and the little ones were captured. The blood witch tracked my bottle to this place. I'll never stop trying to make that right."*

Vaspara believed him.

But she wasn't given a chance to tell him as much in words, for she was being marched through the portal. Journey's end would be where she'd started, but this time she'd be a traitor and a prisoner with all the punishments that would bring.

But Sorac and their drakelings would live.

Perhaps after the Avatars returned to the Magic Realm and dealt the Battle Goddess a great defeat, Vaspara would be freed from her dark prison. And if she were lucky, perhaps Sorac would survive, and they'd be granted a chance to fly through the skies together again, their family sailing the thermals with them.

She could hope.

It was the only thing left to her.

THE END

None of this would have been possible without, you, my readers. You're awesome! Thank You!

Bye for now,
Lisa Blackwood

ABOUT THE AUTHOR

Lisa Blackwood is the author of the bestselling Gargoyle and Sorceress urban fantasy series. Her work has also landed on the Wall Street Journal and the USA Today Bestseller lists as part of the Dominion Rising Anthology. When she's not reading and writing, she also enjoys gardening and spending time with her horse and her dogs.

At present, she grudgingly lives in a small town in Southern Ontario, though she would much rather live deep in a dark forest, surrounded by majestic old-growth trees. Since she cannot live her fantasy, she decided to write fantasy instead.

BOOKS BY LISA BLACKWOOD

Gargoyle & Sorceress

Dawn of the Sorceress

Sorceress Awakening

Sorceress Rising

Sorceress Hunting

Sorceress at War

Sorceress Enraged

Legacy of the Sorceress

Sorcery & Firedrakes

Scion of the Sorceress

Sorceress Eternal

In Deception's Shadow Series (Epic Fantasy Romance)

Betrayal's Price

Herd Mistress

Maiden's Wolf

Death's Queen

The Prince's Gryphon (forthcoming)

Ishtar's Legacy Series (Epic Fantasy Romance)

Ishtar's Blade

The Blade's Beginning (short story)

Blade's Honor

Blade's Destiny

The Blade's Shadow

First Queen of the Gryphons

The King of the Anunnaki (forthcoming)

The Anunnaki's Blade (forthcoming)

Huntress vs Huntsman (Epic Fantasy Romance)

Master of the Hunt

Night Huntress

Dragon Archer

Soul Mage (forthcoming)